I0738067

Bishop Myriel

in his own words

Alfred J. Garrotto

Wisdom of *Les Miserables*
Book 2

WLM
Books

Bishop Myriel: In His Own Words

Wisdom of *Les Miserables* Series
Book 2

978-0-578-64441-7
First Edition

© 2020 by Alfred J. Garrotto

Cover photo © Matthew T. Rader
(used with permission)

Most Scripture quotations are from the
Christian Community Bible
Catholic Pastoral Edition
© 2000 by Bernardo Hurault

To Victor Hugo

i devour your work
study your life
search your soul
and mine

whence your gift
to pen a gospel
peer into the soul
of good and evil

divine one
steps forward
confessing shyly
blame me

To Esther, Monica, Cristina and Dominic
who continue to inspire me and own my heart

Contents

The Ghostwriter's Preface

I claim the title, *ghostwriter*, with great humility and esteem for Bishop Myriel, Victor Hugo's catalyst character in *Les Miserables*. Basing this novel on an already well-known and beloved fictional protagonist posed a challenge, to say the least. My original design for this work consisted of each chapter containing three segments: *fiction* (filling out the character of Bishop Charles Francois Myriel); followed by a *nonfiction* essay (reflecting on my own personal experience of dealing with life-situations similar to those in the bishop's life); and closing each chapter with a *poem* relevant to the chapter's theme.

Nearing completion of the first draft, I secured the input from a select group of early readers. One of them, Honey O'Leary, suggested that I simply focus on Bishop Myriel's story and figure out some other vehicle for my personal musings and poems. Honey's suggestion struck a chord of "rightness" within me. My only concern was doubt that I would have enough material in the bishop's part to produce more than a short booklet. To find the answer, I stripped the manuscript of all personal musings. To my surprise, I still had a respectable page count for a stand-alone book. I also discovered in this process that I had written an uncluttered novel.

The book you now hold in your hand is . . . a novel, my fictionalized story of the fictional character Bishop Myriel, his life and times. I apologize to the great Victor Hugo, who might read this in "author heaven" and not be pleased. I'll have to face that when Hugo and I meet some day on that common ground (or cloud).

Why This Story?

In the dramatic stage adaptation of *Les Miserables*, with music by Claude-Michel Schönberg, French lyrics by Jean-Marc Natel and in English by Herbert Kretzmer, Bishop Myriel appears early in Act I for barely a few minutes. During that brief encounter with mendicant Jean Valjean, the bishop bestows upon the wild-looking parolee the inherited Myriel family treasures (silver dinnerware and candlesticks). Before they part ways on stage, the bishop spontaneously "commissions" Valjean with a new calling in life:

"Jean Valjean, my brother: you belong no longer to evil, but to good. It is your soul that I am buying for you. I withdraw it from dark thoughts and from the spirit of perdition, and I give it to God!"

With that surprising and confusing revelation, the
bishop withdraws from the stage not to be seen again
until Valjean's deathbed scene when he appears to the
dying man as in a vision.

How different the scene in Hugo's original! The *first
lines* of that sprawling epic present Bishop Myriel front and
center as a major player in the story:

*In 1815, M. Charles Francois Myriel was Bishop of
D____. He was a man of seventy-five and had
occupied the bishopric of D____ since 1806.*

Fantine, Book the First, Chapter I, Myriel

In the commission scene, the bishop's final words to
Valjean are:

*"Remember this my brother, you will use this precious
silver to become an honest man. By the witness of the
martyrs, by the Passion and the Blood, God has raised
you out of darkness; I have saved your soul for God."*

Soon after being released, however, Valjean robs Petit
Gervais, a lone child on a deserted road. Suddenly, he
recalls the bishop's mandate (in this abbreviated form):

"... you have promised me to become an honest man. I am purchasing your soul; I withdraw it from the spirit of perversity and give it to God Almighty."

Myriel and Valjean never meet again, at least not until Jean Valjean lies on his deathbed. Hugo describes that scene as follows:

The portress had come up and was looking through the half-open door. The physician motioned her away, but he could not prevent that good, zealous woman from crying to the dying man before she went"

"Do you want a priest?"

"I have one," answered Jean Valjean.

And, with his finger, he seemed to designate a point above his head, where, you would have said, he saw someone. It is probable that the Bishop was indeed a witness of his death-agony.

Over the century-and-a half of the original novel's existence, a number of abridged versions of the 1,200-plus pages have appeared. Some publishers made an editorial decision to abridge the text. In doing so, they generally omit the statement that Bishop Myriel was in the process of writing a book on the topic of Christian duty. I am grateful for Charles E. Wilbour's unabridged

English translation (1862, the very year of the novel's
first publication. Wilbour includes Hugo's detailed,
Scripture-based outline of the bishop's opus-to-be.
Random House's Modern Library Edition of Wilbour's
translation (2000) filled that important gap.

We are told by Victor Hugo himself that the work
remained unfinished. The bishop's detailed outline captured my imagination and launched me on a twenty-year
inner quest that has resulted, finally, in this historical
novel. Probing *Les Miserables'* expansive spirit has become
my passion.

I can only hope that I serve the good bishop well by
attempting to channel his spirit. Called to this work, I
dare to offer what I call a *first draft manuscript* of Bishop
Myriel's book. In doing so, I have done my best to
preserve *Duty*'s outline as created by the original author.
First, I offer a set of reflections on themes given birth in
Myriel's rich and fertile prayer life. Then, I offer my
rendering of the book the bishop outlined but never
completed.

Part the First: The Duties of All addresses key virtues
applicable to all people of good will. Part the Second:
Duties According to One's Life offers insight into
common obligations applicable to roles being lived by
specific segments of Christian and secular society.

Throughout, I use a common typeface to convey the
Bishop's interior thoughts—his ponderings—and French
Script MT to indicate what he committed to paper.

Where applicable and to maintain a connection with the original story, I employ citations at the head of most chapters from Hugo's original text or relevant citations from the New Testament.

I invite and welcome your feedback.

Les Miserables

Victor Hugo's Preface

So long as there shall exist, by reason of law and customs, a social condemnation, which, in the face of civilization, artificially creates hells on earth, and complicates a destiny that is divine, with human frailty; so long as the three problems of the age—the degradation of man by poverty, the ruin of woman by starvation, and the dwarfing of childhood by physical and spiritual night—are not solved; as long as, in certain regions, social asphyxia shall be possible; in other words, and from a yet more extended point of view, so long as ignorance and misery remain on earth, books like this cannot be useless.

Hauteville House, Isle of Guernsey, 1862

The Bishop "had his own way of looking at things. I think he derived it from the Gospel."
      – Victor Hugo

The Beauty of Goodness

[Myriel's sister, Baptistine] had never been pretty; her whole life, which had been a succession of pious works, had produced upon her a kind of transparent whiteness, and in growing old she had acquired what may be called the beauty of goodness.

Fantine, Book the First, Chapter I, M. Myriel: An Upright Man

I am compelled by grace to explore a phenomenon I have observed with awe over the course of my lifetime. We Frenchmen are obsessed with beauty. The ancient Greeks were as appearance-consumed as upper class culture is today. Yet, they had the insight to peg the root of beauty to the word, ὥρα (in Koine, their common dialect). It meant "being one's hour," an interesting linkage to be sure. Beauty, then, knows "what time it is" or better perhaps "knowing who I am and who I am not." My personal mandate as a human, then, is to know my true relationship with every person I encounter, at each stage of my journey and all the individual days that comprise that journey.

I offer my dear sister Baptistine as a model of virtuous living. The call to recognize the "beauty of goodness," however, applies not only to those having a lifelong resume of virtue. I have witnessed beauty's goodness at life's earliest stages. A toddler knows no other way of being than "in the moment," even as the child grows and changes from week to week. A mother holding her child in her arms, searches beyond that moment for hints of the emerging man or woman in their maturity. I suspect that, within every parent there resides an unspoken awareness that they may not live to see their children fulfill their God-given destiny.

I have witnessed the beauty of goodness in teenage years, when it easily suffers displacement along the meandering path to maturity. I pay attention when I hear of any child, teenager, or young adult taken too soon by illness or tragedy. Also, when I hear of young soldiers sacrificing their precious lives on the desecrated altars of their elders' self-serving wars. Parents and friends remark, "He was such a fine young man, always ready to assist someone," or "He was too good for this world." My heart cries, "No! The world needs such young, idealistic men to stay alive, to make their mark upon our shattered society!" Some of us live our way into beauty. Others suffer their way to it. I think of patients I have known in our neighboring hospital whose clear eyes glow with inner light.

The beauty of goodness is like that hidden treasure Jesus spoke of in Matthew 13:44:

> *The kingdom of heaven is like a treasure, hidden in a field. The one who finds it, buries it again; and so happy is he, that he goes and sells everything he has, in order to buy that field.*

When I discover goodness, be it for a moment or longer, I rejoice in its native beauty and bask in its bright light. So inspired, I take quill pen in hand. I lay no claim, on earth or before God, to poetic aptitude.

At those times when, I hear the call, I should say "challenge"—of the muse, I dare to express my heart in the fewest possible syllables. In doing so, I take comfort in knowing that no other eyes will see—and, God forbid, judge, my verse.

The Beauty of Goodness

i see goodness
in a mother's smile
a helping hand
a loving heart

i find goodness
in a kind word
a silent shrine
sunrise aglow

chancing upon the
beauty of goodness
i catch my breath
stand in awe

Husband and Priest

Was [Myriel], in the midst of these distractions, these affections which absorbed his life, suddenly smitten with one of those mysterious and terrible blows which sometimes overwhelm, by striking to his heart, a man whom public catastrophes would not shake, by striking at his existence and his fortune? No one could have told: all that was known was, that when he returned from Italy, he was a priest.

Fantine. Book the First, Chapter I, M. Myriel

8

I am a stranger neither to grief nor its accompanying sense of disorientation. Two periods of severe loss and subsequent paralysis stand out in my life among others of similar but lesser rank.

The first occurred when I, along with my young bride, whom I adored, fled our beloved France in fear of losing our freedom, perhaps even our lives. Like others of our social class, my father trusted in prevailing aristocratic confidence that the Summer Revolution of 1789 would run its bloodthirsty course only to die under the firm heel of our divinely ordered and sanctioned monarchy. "Other uprisings have failed. So will this one," our noble families assured each other. This conviction posed as divine wisdom among my elders and many of my peers. How quickly the centuries-old *ancien regime* fell into the rubble of history! And what a bloody crash that was.

My father saw what lay ahead and urged me to flee with my new wife. It was then that I emigrated—no, fled—from France for the safety and relative anonymity of Italy. The journey proved arduous, more so for my beloved than for me. Traversing hazardous mountain trails, we thanked God we had no children yet to suffer this hardship with us. Upon arriving at last in Rome, weary and disoriented, we found welcome and relief. The climate of sunny days and temperate nights, the very air we breathed filled our senses and our hearts with, music, poetry, and art. To our pleasure and surprise, the local citizenry accepted us young, upper class refugees with open-armed warmth, easing somewhat the hardship and uncertainty of our exile. What pleased me most was the Holy City's ability to elevate my beloved's spirit. On our own for the first time, we experienced a sense of unaccustomed freedom from familial and societal oversight. Recalling those days from the passage of distant decades, how seamlessly we settled into our new life. The intensity of our lovemaking generated hope that our comfortable home might soon welcome the first of what we hoped would be many children. Our emotional uplift proved short-lived. Our much-desired infant failed to appear. I accepted our temporary deprivation as God's will. Not so my bride. She suffered that disappointing lacuna more and more as the first twelve months rolled into two more years, then more.

Beneath the laughter and eager passion, spurring us blissfully forward each day, an unwelcome sadness crept into each goodbye, every good night kiss, and passionate embrace. By the time I allowed myself to accept the truth of her failing lungs, she was already hearing the call to embark on another, final journey. This one she must make without me. Standing as on a deserted dock, I watched her drift away to a distant shore, as yet off limits to me. God knows, I prayed more than once to be allowed to exchange my life for hers, or at least to accompany her into Paradise. Neither came to be.

Peering into her open grave, I stepped off a cliff with no protruding tree limb to break my fall—no out-stretched hand to grasp and rescue me from freefall into dark and empty space. For more than a year after her passing, I wallowed in solitary bereavement in that lovely but increasingly desolate land.

Often, I thought of returning to France to grieve in the understanding company of family and friends. I simply could not muster strength for a journey home. How could I leave my beloved alone in that foreign resting place? What to do, lost as I was?

With danger still in the stormy winds at home, I had burned, I thought, all bridges to past entitlement. In accepting exile, I believed that sharing life with my dear wife and our children would compensate for our shared loss of family and homeland.

My frayed bond and tepid devotion to our Catholic faith seemed my only commonality with society in the heart of the Italian peninsula.

Into that void stepped one with whom I had, until that moment, enjoyed a mere casual acquaintance. Jesus Christ. In the year following my wife's death, I began attending weekly, then daily Mass in the stately church of Santa Francesca di Roma. I had never heard of this holy woman who died in 1440, but I soon learned that death cut a deep swath through her home, as well. She lost two children to plague.

I felt at home among the congregants, widows most of them, clothed in black mourning from shawled heads to sandaled feet. Among them, too, were grateful young mothers cuddling olive-skinned babes in their arms. I averted my gaze at first. The stabbing pain of childlessness filled my being with emptiness and regret. Among the few men in attendance, I was the youngest. Nonetheless, each day my spirit opened a tiny bit more to the community around me.

Like the first explorers on the American continents, I discovered and mapped an unexpected source of comfort in prayer—real prayer—and devotional practices with meaning exceeding the rote recitations of my childhood experience. I found solace in meditations on the sorrowful mysteries of the rosary and the stations of the cross, both of which invited personal sharing in Jesus' suffering and death. Suffering. I knew that unwelcome guest too well. The fog of personal grief narrowed my vision of both human and divine love.

One particular Sunday, before the celebrant preached his sermon, he read from the sixteenth chapter of St. Luke. Jesus told a story about a beggar named Lazarus, who camped at an unnamed rich man's gate. The master of the house paid no attention whatsoever to that poor soul. The beggar might have been a broken fencepost, for all the rich man cared.

With a sudden jolt, the Lord opened my eyes and my heart that day. *"I am that man!"* came a cry from my damaged inner self. Not Lazarus, the beggar, to be sure. I identified with the well-fed aristocrat who came and went unconcerned about the odor and nuisance of suffering beyond my door. Shame swept through me, but grace shone a beam of light upon my darkened spirit. I restrained myself from standing up at that very moment and confessing to the priest and congregation, "I am he, that man! Forgive me, good people."

A new and once-alien life plan forced itself upon my attention, a plan more foreign to me than Italy's people and their earthy philosophy of life. How could I have known?

This vision of my future had waited with divine patience for my spirit to discover and acknowledge my new awareness. What God had in store for me surpassed in joy and satisfaction my privileged upbringing. It exceeded even—*could it be possible?*—my love for my late wife, whom I cherished in death more than the flowery fragrant Roman air I breathed and delighted in.

Overnight, I became aware of beggars—mothers, fathers, children, many of them ill—who staked their claims outside the church doors. I had formerly ignored

them, passing unseeing on my way into and away from
Mass. I responded to the grace of understanding that
those huddled outside suffered a far greater pain than my
own. They fed their families on crumbs tossed to them
by a few generous Massgoers—some of whom existed
themselves at the near edge of poverty.

Following my miraculous awakening, I found myself
one morning sweating in a dark, airless confessional
kneeling on a rough wooden plank. I needed guidance
to face a new and unfamiliar temptation—the call to, of
all things . . . "priesthood?" I laughed aloud the first time
I allowed the concept to take flight in speech.

Having put my Lord's stalking grace into words for
the first time, I dared not look back. I had abandoned
family and friends in France to avoid the guillotine. Life
had compounded my loss in widowhood. Now, with my
beloved safely home in heaven, I buried myself no longer
in her grave but in the *Summa Theologica* of St. Thomas
Aquinas. Sometime after my ordination, I received an
invitation from the Cardinal Archbishop of Paris to
return to the land of my birth.

Eschewing Paris, still a hotbed of political intrigue
and self-serving betrayal, I sought permission to settle in
a less conspicuous region in Southern France. To
abbreviate my story, I became a parish priest and knew I
had finally found my elusive true self.   I looked forward

to dying a happy man after a lifetime of ministry among the poorest of God's poor. It was not to be.

The family name, Myriel, exposed my hiding place. I received a summons from Paris to shepherd the diocese of Digne, still sufficiently distant from the contentious civil and ecclesiastical politics of the time. I relished my episcopal ministry, but never saw myself as more than a simple parish priest but one having broader responsibility. I expected to live out my days in Digne and die contented, with my dear older sister—and self-appointed guard dog—Baptistine in prayer at my bedside.

I recall during my first year as bishop complaining to my spiritual director, "I am always being interrupted during prayer and when I should be preparing a sermon; most especially during meals." That gentle and compassionate doctor of souls reflected on my words with closed eyes, seeming to await instructions from above. He looked at me—rather, *into* me—and spoke with gentleness and respect words I have never forgotten and have done my best to live by, "Monseigneur, it is not my place to lecture you on the nature and vicissitudes of priestly ministry."

"Oh, please do," I begged. "Apart from my sister, I have no one who feels free enough to shine a holy light on my faults."

"In that case," my confessor continued, "the earthly ministry of our Lord was one of constant interruption." He cited several examples from the Gospels. "I dare say, Your Excellency, interruption *is* your ministry."

I have lived by the light of that truth ever since.

Again, I feel called to play the amateur poet and pen this private summary of my meditation . . .

In God's Time

in early manhood
dimly choosing
with light available
life's unmarked plan
obedient to half-sight
declaring complete
my unformed life
in painful light
of naked day

truth revealed
confusion exposed
holy self-deception
a whispered "follow me"
revealed a path
half-truth's other
reborn imaginings
once-shunned yearnings
offered resurrection
former patterns renewed
not abandoned
sideroads explored
the old in me reborn
unknown peace set free

Imagine

[Myriel] contemplated the grandeur, the presence of God; the eternity of the future, strange mystery; the eternity of the past, mystery yet more strange; all the infinities deep hidden in every direction about him; and, without assaying to comprehend the incomprehensible, he saw it. He did not study God; he was dazzled by the thought.

Fantine, Book the First, Chapter XIII,
What He Believed

During my years of study for the priesthood in Italy, I learned a great deal about the "science" of God. We called it Theology. After some time, but prior to ordination, I discovered how little I knew of the immeasurable nature of Divine Love—and my place within that universe. What I had lacked to that point in my life was not faith. Nor was commitment lacking. I came to discern that the Lord had showered me with gifts—both wonderfully joyful and infinitely sad. Among the most valuable of those blessings I cherish imagination—the capacity to "see" beyond the span of my physical sight.

At some unmarked point along the way, whether in chapel or in lecture hall—I cannot recall—I heard your voice within me, Lord. You whispered, "Don't let them fool you, Charles. I am not a specimen to examine and study in a lecture hall. Nor will you discover my true Self within the pages of leather-bound tomes purporting to explain. . . yes, explain all that is known about me. In vain do you search for me, your Creator and Savior, within the countless Canons they require you to memorize."

"If not in these learned texts of Holy Mother Church," I asked, "where shall I search. Where might I find your true Self—and mine?"

"Follow me," came the reply.

I waited for further word . . . nothing.

The next afternoon, after a dull, morning-long lecture on the morality of an array of devious sexual acts, a barely audible whisper directed me to visit the multishrined Cimitero Santo Sepolcro, where my beloved wife lay in peaceful rest. Since the day I left her there in that lonely place to spend her first night without me at her side, I had not the strength of spirit to force myself back to that sad shrine. I often felt my soul too had parted from my flesh, leaving my body on earth to perform the functions of a half-living being.

A guilty disease halted me within view of her headstone.

"Must I, my Lord?"

Feeble question. What choice had I but to obey? Tucking up my black soutane, I approached and sat at her side on a smooth gravel path.

"It is I, beloved. Forgive me. I could not come bef—"

"*Could* not?"

She spoke to my heart in tender admonishment but with a hint of whimsy, teasing me in that sweet voice and lilting tone I so cherished. My heart leapt within my chest. I turned expecting to see her alive again, standing behind me, ready to be taken home. Ready to resume our quest for children and lifelong communion in mutual love.

"I could have, of course," I admitted, "but I dared not lest I lay down beside you and succumb to fatal grief."

"I understand, my love. I do. I approve of this new course your life path has chosen."

A tidal wave of gratitude rushed through my being. In a flash, all became clear. I understood at last where to find Divine Love personified. Yes, I needed to study systematic theology and learn the countless laws our Church had amassed over centuries of lived experience of virtue and vice, but I would not be fooled again by a misguided priority of truths.

I vowed from that day forward to rejoice in the lesson learned at my beloved's gravesite. In season and out, I would seek the Primary font of God's love, the limitless treasure trove of divinity. My field of plentiful harvest would be the people entrusted to my care as priest of the Church, especially those suffering the travails of inherited poverty, illness, and fatalistic acceptance of repression.

In that graced moment, I also understood I could never find contentment in the role of what some called a "sacristy priest," one who rarely strayed beyond the boundaries of church property. Somehow, I must take my daily search for the one true God into the dirty, polluted streets of the most far-flung outposts of France; to the hovels of the poor and to prisoners locked away and forgotten until the date arrived for release or death at the guillotine. I opened my soul to the possibility of finding my vocation fulfilled in mission territories far from my homeland, among a people who, without full awareness, thirsted for knowledge and experience of the Crucified One.

It came as a further shock and affront to my aristocratic family in Paris, but not to me, when the Good Shepherd of all called me to the politically insignificant southeastern city of Digne and its surrounding mountain villages. This has been my field of harvest—my life— these many years. I find both God and contentment in service to the largely forgotten people of my region; and yes, especially to the Jean Valjeans of this world. For all of which I thank you, Lord Jesus, with all my being.

Though I lay no claim to the title, poet, I do find at times that my daily contemplations cry out for expression in the shorthand of verse. These few lines serve as reminders of those occasional revelations— points of light and wisdom.

They break through walls of mental dimness and lack of understanding that often cloud my perspective on what is true and important in life. So, again I respond to my spirit's partner in prayer, the written word.

Imagine

i search for
questions not answers
in hope of vision pure
i imagine a God
beyond imagining
a love unimagined
i imagine today
and tomorrow's morrow
with eyes of hope
vision fresh-renewed
brighter days reveal
enemies find peace
i open myself
to unimagined

assurance of hope
conviction of life
as yet unseen
. . . imagine that

Listening

The senator . . . was a clever man, who had made his own way, heedless of those things which present obsta.-cles, and which are called conscience, sworn faith, justice, duty: he had marched straight to his goal, without once flinching in the line of his advancement and his interest. He was an old attorney, softened by success; not a bad man by any means, who rendered all the small services in his power to his sons, his sons-in-law, his relations, and even to his friends, having wisely seized upon, in life, good sides, good opportunities, good windfalls. Everything else seemed to him very stupid. He was intelligent, and just sufficiently educated to think himself a disciple of Epicurus; while he was, in reality, only a product of Pigault-Lebrun. He laughed willingly and pleasantly over infinite and eternal things, and at the "crotchets [quarter notes] of that good old fellow the Bishop." He even sometimes laughed at him with an amiable authority in the presence of M. Myriel himself, who listened to him.

Fantine, Book the First, Chapter VIII,
After Dinner Philosophy

This evening, I dined with the Senator, a Count, and therefore a man of, dare I say, some prominence in our region. Before retiring, let me reprise salient points of our conversation. In so doing, I feel the urgent need for self-examen during which I shall explore an ever-difficult aspect of my ministry, that of listening. Not simply hearing but full listening and doing so *without judgment* —"Ay, there is the rub," saith Hamlet.

After my host's servant had regaled us with a tasty dessert and a glass of golden apricot liqueur, the Senator expounded with great conviction on—in this order—the stupidity of self-denial, the death of what he called "moral conscience," and the irrationality of believing in life after death. He concluded with what he desired to be this nail-in-the-coffin question, with the goal, it appeared, of teaching me something he expected me to affirm without dissent or further comment.

"And upon death we shall see God, Monsieur Bishop?" Without pause, he settled the matter for all time. "A monstrous myth! Take it from me, man's only morrow is everlasting night."

He paused, expecting me, it seemed, to play the role of ignorant fish snapping at his bait by countering with impotent platitudes. Thus confirming his infallibility . . . and my naiveté.

Instead, I remained silent and poured a few ounces from the elegant decanter into my crystal goblet. Its etchings caught a flicker of candlelight sending a rainbow of color splashing across the white linen tablecloth. This colorful gift reminded me that truth shares its wisdom generously and democratically among many hues of light, be they lustrous or dim.

Lacking an opponent, the Senator's mood softened. "Lest you think me too harsh, I do grant you this much, the concept of an almighty God performs a service for the many barefooted, the wandering vendors, all the wretches of the world who clog our narrow lanes and markets. Yes, I grant you, the concept of a 'good God' is beneficial for those unfortunate people." He leaned forward and, with a conspiratorial wink, sought to include me in his cabal. "I mean of course, Monsieur Bishop, those benighted souls born to a class beneath that of the two of us."

I weighed my host's opinions, testing each against my own. Again, I did not respond to his thesis, neither to approve nor dispute. My only comment was, "My dear Senator, although the rich and powerful have privileged access to your philosophy, I find it interesting that you make room within your predestined system to allow the poor their God."

"Exactly! As I surmised, Monsieur Bishop, you are among those too rare churchmen who understand the way this world truly functions."

A heaviness pressed upon my chest at his broad indictment, too often true, I fear. "I do, indeed, understand how things . . . truly are. Believe me, I do."

The count's porcelain clock rested in secure comfort upon an elegantly carved mantle. Its golden hands had swept past my usual bedtime. After thanking my host for the opulent meal and excellent wines, I made my way homeward through the dark streets of Digne. The only sounds at this time of night were those of awakened dogs, barking complaints as their bishop passed their bishop passed their homes, his stomach full, his heart heavy laden.

The farther I retreated from my dinner host, the louder the voice of my critical self chastised me. "Charles, you sat there while that man spewed his philosophical ramblings, his condescending pseudo-theological assumptions."

"Be still," I countered. I had no need to come away with a blue ribbon, as if our exchanges constituted an official debate, with a clear winner and humbled loser.

In truth, the Senator had presented me with a rare opportunity to hear a clear exposition of the split-level world in which I live and minister. Someday, my turn will come. Then, I shall share with my friend that I, too, live by a moral compass, the North of whose magnetic field is the Creator and Sustainer of all that exists plus humanity itself. Pools of wisdom give birth to thought and subsequent action and works for the betterment of one and all within the human network. I embrace and celebrate that wisdom. I endeavor each day to make it my own. When, however, the birthing waters of the Spirit foster strife and division, it is my calling to apply the healing salve of love to victims of the Evil One.

For tonight, I will remember the Senator-Count in my prayers. But first, let me share my fading thoughts in a few scratched lines of verse . . .

Wisdom Not Words

we pour out words

in swollen streams

untiring of their sound

so long as ours they be

listening's a different skill

perfected in silence

demanding discipline

oft' with meager gain

no reward in
in learned repartee
wisdom's humble womb
births life well lived

Prayer

Prayer, the celebration of the offices of religion, almsgiving, the consolation of the afflicted, the cultivation of a bit of land, fraternity, frugality, hospitality, renunciation, confidence, study, work, filled every day of his life. Filled is exactly the word; certainly. the Bishop's day was quite full to the brim, of good words and good deeds. Nevertheless, it was not complete if cold or rainy weather prevented his passing an hour or two in his garden before going to bed, and after the two women had retired. It seemed to be a sort of rite with him, to prepare himself for slumber by meditation in the presence of the grand spectacles of the nocturnal heavens. . . .

At such moments, while he offered his heart at the hour when nocturnal flowers offer their perfume, illuminated like a lamp amid the starry night, as he poured himself out in ecstasy in the midst of the universal radiance of creation, he could not have told himself, probably, what was passing in his spirit; he felt something take its flight from him, and something descend into him.

Mysterious exchange of the abysses of the soul with the abysses of the universe!

Fantine, Book the First, Chapter XIII,
What He Believed

When you pray, do not use a lot of words, as the pagans do, for they hold that the more they say, the more chance they have of being heard. Do not be like them. Your Father knows what you need, even before you ask him. This, then, is how you should pray: "Our Father in heaven. . . ."

Matthew 6:7-9

A young priest of my diocese, not far removed in time from his day of ordination, asked me if I prayed a great deal. I replied, "Not a great deal"—but, after a moment's reflection, I could not help but smile and add—"on second thought, I am always praying."

Let me offer some background. Out of the seemingly impenetrable emptiness of my youth, our Good Lord blessed me with the love of a faith-filled bride, a young woman I confess even now to be an angelic presence at my side. By the grace of that same God, I possessed the good sense not to rebel against my father's decision.

Too soon afterwards, I found myself alone again, a widower in a foreign land. Entombed in my despair, I experienced a hitherto unknown feeling of childlike wonder at life, in all its public and private manifestations.

At first, I felt guiltily disloyal to my absent bride. Gradually, though, I recognized the hand of God in this dawning phase of my religious revival.

Revival. An apt word.

Being born again, not in flesh but in spirit. I had all but denied the possibility of a loving, faithful God.

The source of my unaccustomed awe? A dawning awareness of an expansive God who, rather than dismissing me as lost, daily surprised me with the beauty of the Roman people and the wondrous beauty of ancient artifacts and churches I had hitherto barely taken time to notice.

In the depths of my rootlessness, Jesus the Christ stepped from the shadows revealing a surprising depth of compassion for this lost soul. He opened my heart to a love even more satisfying, if that were possible, than that which I had known as husband and devoted life companion. My Creator-God, whom I had believed to be no more than a distant presence somewhere in the expanse of our shared universes, encompassed me within a divine embrace including every living and inanimate being, seen and unseen, on earth, in the heavens, and beyond.

During my years of study for ordination to the priesthood, I felt a growing need to attend to my emerging, indwelling God. As my concept and intimate experience of divinity expanded, I grew to believe in and pray to a divine lover of limitless capacity for forgiveness, one determined not to lose a single human soul. This conviction did not please my theology professors, who thinly veiled their suspicion of my orthodoxy and fitness for Holy Orders. I survived by the grace of God and— I'm sure—my status as one born into the French upper class. I suspected then and still believe that the latter reason weighed heavily in my favor.

After taking Holy Orders and my subsequent installation as Bishop of Digne, some among the clergy and upper classes of society questioned, not so privately, the quality of my seminary training. Absent from my pulpit and confessional was any trace of hellfire and damnation. Jesus, after all, never encountered a soul he deemed beyond redemption. Early in my ministry, the conversion of Paul the Apostle, recorded in the ninth chapter of the Acts of the Apostles, became for me the most authentic Christian model of Divine Mercy. And proof that our benevolent Savior never gave up on any human being. Confident in my assessment of the divine, I have searched for evidence of our trinitarian God amid the same unlikely people and places Jesus did. Our blessed Lord lived among the poor, chose as close companions and friends those regarded as outcasts whom the upper strata of religious society callously marginalize for their supposed sins—whether personal or inherited. He assured those branded as unclean by rigid interpretations of Hebraic Law that everything and everyone issuing from the Creator is and can only be, without exception and forever, "very good" (Genesis 1:10). Even so-called lesser beings of the animal world deserve my loving care.

One day a large, hairy spider crossed my path as Baptistine and I sat on our garden bench—my favorite prayer shrine in clement weather. This widely despised creature of God lacked the natural beauty of, say, a lily in bloom. Who but a very few would ever pause in awe of this creature's transcendent splendor? Observing that spider, who lived simply in silence by laws instilled by its creator, moved me deeply.

"Poor thing," I said to my multilegged neighbor, "it is no fault of yours that you are despised."

But I digress. Again.

At times, I have difficulty distinguishing between inspiration and distraction.

Ongoing dialog with God is the lifeblood of a full spiritual life. In cherished silent hours, I contemplate the grandeur of my God. When discouragement and self-doubt cloud my vision, I ask my Father, His Son, and the all-wise Holy Spirit to enfold me in a faith-affirming embrace. It is in daily prayer—through each hour of every day—that I receive affirmation, encouragement, and inspiration to continue serving the portion of the Good Shepherd's flock allotted to me, most of them struggling to feed and shelter their growing families.

I have listened as some of my fellow preachers speak of prayer in terms of "duty," and as our "obligation" to

God. I prefer to describe prayer as a form of "gratitude"— for the favors of existence, community, unconditional love. Knowing that our God cherishes each of us "no matter what" alters the spiritual environment of the divine-human relationship.

Whatever pastoral skills I possess and bring to ministry I have inherited from the example of Jesus found, most notably, in his brilliant parables. On this night, I kneel beside my bed and call to mind Jesus' tale of the loving father in Luke 15. This good and kindly man had truly lost *both* of his sons. Just in different ways. One to a misguided search for the elusive pleasures of so-called "freedom," the other to bitter-hearted resentment.

This and others of Jesus' many teaching stories reveal a God desirous of my extended time and single-minded attention. Limiting my prayer life to the realm of episcopal duty would only condemn me, I fear, to a life of spiritual boredom and ultimate failure. In contrast, prayer rooted in gratitude, otherness, and universal love brings salutary, if mostly disguised, benefits. Intimate communication opens my heart to welcome strangers, forgive injuries, and hope for what may seem, to the spiritually nearsighted, hopeless.

And so, I pray.

Before retiring, I must again put in verse the words

rising in my heart. Experience has taught me, if I
postpone till the morrow, my mental eraser might
wipe the slate clean. Another sign of advancing years.
The following lines are for my eyes only. I would be
embarrassed to share or impose them upon others.

And So I Pray

i cannot blame peter
forbidding your washing
nor judas selling out
you came to play
by your rules
wine from water
bread into body
wine to blood
you thought them fools
they had their pride

paul understood but
never touched your flesh
had you knelt before him
with basin and towel
he too might forbid
what about me
submit peter-like
run like judas
some of both in me
i dare not boast
and so i pray

Gardening

Sometimes [Bishop Myriel] used a spade in his garden, and sometimes he read and wrote. He had but one name for these two kinds of labor; he called them gardening.

Fantine, Book the First, Chapter V,
How Monseigneur Bienvenu
Made His Cassock Last So Long

At his feet something to cultivate and gather; above his head something to study and meditate upon; a few flowers on the earth, and all the stars in the sky.

Fantine, Book the First, Chapter XIII,
What He Believed

Since settling in Digne, my first permanent home since ordination to the priesthood, I have grown to love having my own garden to cultivate. Through our generally mild winters, compared to the surrounding mountains, I look forward to nature's annual revival.

Before turning the first spade of eager earth, I bless my plot of fertile French soil, inviting its resurrection from the long and frigid nap. On welcoming spring afternoons, passersby stop to pay respects and watch me at work. Some kindly souls offer to take my place. I decline with a blessing and sincere gratitude for thinking of their aging shepherd's wellbeing.

Each square meter teems with possibility to produce and sustain life in myriad varieties. My horticultural technique is first to mark off and divide the sections; then to awaken dormant soil. Immersing my winter-smoothed palms into pregnant earth quickens my anticipation of the unique beauty of each individual root and the beneficial sustenance our God predestines my garden to produce. Kneeling in this open-air patch of soil, I feel at one with my Creator, more so than at any other time, with the exception of when sacred words, not sweaty palms, make present in Eucharist our Lord and Savior, Jesus, the living Christ.

My heart swells with holy pride as spring cultivation

yields blooms. I marvel that they appear and thrive despite flaws in my amateur horticultural skills. Toiling in warming weather, my woolen black soutane adds a level of difficulty other gardeners do not share. Stopping to mop my brow, I anticipate the joy of reading, praying, and writing in the shade of blossoming fruit-bearing trees.

I am not gifted with facility at other art forms, although I admit to carrying a passable tune in Gregorian Chant, with its fewer notes and simpler melodic arrangements. I lay no claim to skill at poetry, yet some too-kind souls have said that my sermons have the lilt of poetic verse. I thank them, admitting to my true self that their words innocently stretch the truth.

Are we as humans the universe's first, last, and only hope of preserving nature, as we know it? I have lived through catastrophic wars and revolutions, during which the weapons of self-serving power have destroyed precious natural resources along with irreplaceable human lives. I fear the result of power's rejection of man's caretaker trust over the Almighty's natural gifts, ours to preserve and protect since Adam and Eve shared the unimaginable pleasures of the Eden Garden. All theirs to feast on and enjoy, but one—the tree in the middle of the garden on which grew the *only* fruit off-limits to them.

Desiring independence from what they considered a selfish Creator, they partook of that tree, expecting to become gods, coequal to their Maker. That single over-reach sent humankind on a path of self-destruction that continues to this day, and which I have witnessed with my own eyes.

I rejoice in my caretaker role over life forms within my tiny domain, including this plot over which I labor and the patient life forms waiting to fulfill their destiny.

And so, again I write . . .

Mindful

mindful

with attentive

eyes open

heart open

to body spirit

mindful
God-focused
flesh and spirit one
sensing obstacles
to grace to love

mindful
sight in darkness
light within me
wisdom's gold vein
in earthen vessel

mindful
flesh and spirit one
wisdom's treasure pure
a mind
full of peace

An Undesired Relic

A tragic event occurred at Digne. A man was condemned to death for murder. He was a wretched fellow, not exactly educated, not exactly ignorant, who had been a mountebank at fairs and a writer for the public. The town took great interest in the trial. On the eve of the day fixed for the execution of the condemned man, the chaplain of the prison fell ill. A priest was needed to attend the criminal in his last moments. They sent for the curé [pastor]. It seems that he refused to come, saying, "That is no affair of mine. I have nothing to do with that unpleasant task, and with that mountebank. I, too, am ill; and besides, it is not my place." This reply was reported to the Bishop, who said, "Monsieur le Curé is right. It is not his place, it is mine."

Fantine, Book the First, Chapter IV,
Works Answering Words

One afternoon, as I took my daily walk through the central district of Digne, I came upon a certain square I cross according to my accustomed route. I enjoy chatting with shopkeepers and the hardworking farmers from outlying districts, who cart fresh fruits and vegetables and varieties of cheese to market in the open square. Arriving at the plaza that day, my feet became suddenly leaden. Refusing to carry me forward, they forced me to move slowly and along a less familiar side street. Emerging at last on the other side of the central area, all was quiet. Townsfolk passed each other without exchanging a word, a look. In that instant, I came face to face with man's most hideous monster.

Only once before had I experienced the unforgiving guillotine. I suffered lasting trauma to my spirit. Or, perhaps I was in some way the better for it.

I soon learned that a man of my district stood accused of a capital crime and tried before a jury. The magistrate accepted the prosecutor's witnesses as, at least mostly, reliable. The jurors quickly rendered a guilty verdict. The poor soul now faced a sentence of death by the hideous blade.

I knew of this fellow as a juggler of extraordinary talent at local fairs. Unfortunately, he also had a reputation as a mountebank, an unscrupulous con man. The trial, of which I knew little but soon learned too much, took place—perhaps appropriately, in a grim sort of way—in what eyewitnesses told me was a carnival atmosphere. To my attention later that day, was that the local pastor had Declined, claiming ill health. Rumor also had it that someone heard the cleric admit, "I shall have nothing to do with that no-good mountebank."

I confess to deep disappointment that one of my own pastors had failed to respond to a soul in need. Was it not his priestly duty to offer the ministry of the Church to one of his own parishioners, especially in the desperate man's final hour of deep human and spiritual need? I did not care to hear the sordid details of the crime. Nor did I wish, at that moment, to debate the supposed merit of such a monstrous and public end to his life. My every thought went to the one who refused to perform his priestly duty.

By a grace for which I remain grateful to this day, the Holy Spirit came to my rescue, allowing me to view the matter in a different light, a higher, unearthly wisdom. Why had I not seen it before? My focus on the reluctant pastor and his seeming dereliction of duty had clouded my ability to see the truth with spiritual clarity. Rather, had not the failure of clouded vision been mine? The reluctant priest had been correct. Without awareness, he had done me a great service. As the condemned man's bishop, the greater responsibility for his spiritual well-being fell upon me. It was not the local pastor's duty to share that poor soul's final hours but mine.

I had often visited prisoners, offering what counsel

I could, hearing confessions. Typically, my ministry consisted of grasping the man's hand—praying in silence. My ministry on that particular day marked my first descent into the infamous lower dungeons where the hopeless condemned awaited their appointed hour.

The man I found upon entering the dank cell seemed barely human. His shoulders curled forward, as if to protect what little life remained in his heart. His bearded chin pressed against his chest. Drawn-in knees offered feeble protection to his inner organs.

Whether from terror or an understandable despair of God's existence and love, the inmate, who already appeared to be beyond this world's confinement, made no response to the jailer's announcement of my entrance. The guard brought me a low stool on which I sat opposite the condemned man. After a moment during which I staved off my repulsion at the stench of living death, I took the man's filthy, trembling hands in mine. It was not until I called him by name that his eyes opened a slit. The bloodshot specter I beheld wrenched my soul. He had no need of a priest, let alone a bishop. Since he appeared to have no one else in the entire world to care about him or mourn his departure, I became father, mother, brother, sister and friend to this man-forsaken child of our loving, all-merciful God.

Throughout the afternoon and into the night, I spoke to him of jugglers and other circus performers I had seen years ago in Italy. The condemned offered no sign of comprehension. Neither did he pull away or call the guard to remove me from his presence. Instead, he allowed me to enfold his frigid, trembling fingers within my womb-like palms. I could only wonder how long it had been since he had experienced loving human contact.

With deep sadness, I recalled the dire effects caused by deprivation of caring touch. The memory reprised over-whelming feelings that assaulted my spirit in the days following my beloved's death. How I missed her gentle, loving touch! I physically ached at every reminder of our life together.

Without addressing the crime for which the judge had condemned this man, I spoke from the depths of my own faith, "My son, there is nothing a human being can do to lose God's love. Nothing." I quoted Isaiah 1:16, "Though your sins be as scarlet, they will be made white as snow." I then made the sign of the cross over him in absolution. *"Ego te absolvo."*

Still no response.

I abandoned words, even those most sacred. Sitting knee to knee on the stool in front of him, I grasped his hands again and repeated countless *Ave Marias* through the racing night. I wept each time I came to the words, "Pray for us sinners, now . . . and at the hour of our death." With each repetition, the death hour drew closer. I offered the aching stiffness I suffered for his salvation.

In the morning's early hours, consciousness stirred in the motionless one who had remained through the night rigid as petrified wood. First, his fingers trembled to life.

Terror then vanished from his now-open eyes to an extent that I can only call them radiant, like a Paschal Candle casting holy light over a predawn Easter Vigil. The slightest hint of a smile parted his lips. . . . He reached out to me! And we embraced, laughing and weeping together.

When the fated hour arrived, I walked arm-in-arm with my child/brother/friend to the square and up the steps to the block on which the jailers positioned his neck. Ordered to exit the platform, I jostled my way through the sea of jovial gawkers to a spot directly in the condemned man's line of vision. I struggled mightily to maintain my balance in the jostling crowd.

With the blade about to perform its evil work, he who faced death found my eyes and followed my gaze along the line of my elevated arm to the silver pectoral cross I held as high as I could reach toward the waiting heavens. Wanting mine to be the last words he heard in his mercy-poor life, I shouted, "Whom man kills, God restores to life. Your loving Father is waiting for you!

Believe, my son!"

The blade descended true to its mark.

The dead man's blood splashed across the front of my cassock, a sacred if undesired relic of his death, resurrection, and ascension into the loving arms of his crucified-criminal Savior.

The jubilant crowd jostling around me parted like the Red Sea as I staggered away from the scaffolding and flailed my way with neither dignity nor care through the dispersing crowd. Upon reaching my residence, I endured Baptistine's scolding, "I have been so worried, Charles. You were away all night. What was I to think?"

About my blood-stained clothing, she kept silent.

I heaved a sigh and opened my chamber door. "I have been doing what a bishop must do."

I slept the entire day, not peacefully, but achieving some respite. The sight of the blade raised to its highest point had shocked my entire being, body and spirit. Witnessing its rapid descent severed my spirit, as it had that poor fellow's neck. Feared my ability to repair the damage, I placed my trust in our crucified Lord.

Whenever I reprise that horrible scene, it renews my conviction that the only the condemned, now-sainted man, and he alone among the entire cast of characters, rested in peace that very night. I saw it in his eyes when he caught my gaze and beheld the symbol of his salvation, his key to the gates of eternal life.

As for me, it took a long while before I crossed that plaza without feeling ill. Perhaps putting something in verse might help me sort this jumble of fragile emotions.

Undesired Relics

life is a magnet

collecting bits and pieces

of my days nights

gathered on the way

sacred relics some

welcome additions

treasured and stored

in wayside shrines

others not so

a dead man's blood

indelible stain upon

each forms my i-ness

the fabric of my being
be it shrine or shame
no going back
no erasure of facts

partners in salvation
essential stamps
upon my passport
to humanness redeemed

The Bishop Begins Writing His Book

The bishop was busy with his great work on Duty, which unfortunately is left incomplete. He carefully dissected all that the Fathers and Doctors have said on this serious topic. His book was divided into two parts: First, the duties of all; secondly, the duties of each according to his life . . . . He collated with much labor these injunctions into a harmonious whole, which he wished to offer to souls.

Fantine, Book the Second, Chapter II:
Prudence Commended to Wisdom

Duty

Bishop Charles Francois Myriel

Bishop of Digne

(Draft No. 1)

Preface

It is time, urges my angelic muse.

On these pages, by the Grace of God, I embark on a journey of soul to bring to life the Gospel's timeless message and that of Saint Paul, Apostle to the Gentiles. My immediate audience? The people and clergy of our Diocese of Digne. Should it be the will of God for this volume to travel beyond the limits of my vision, to other parts of our beloved France (perhaps beyond), I pray that my words will speak to the hearts of those unknown to me, believers and unbelievers alike. My chosen topic is Duty. On its face, not an attractive subject.

The human spirit flinches at the very thought and solemn utterance of the word. It is both a challenge and a pleasure to offer a wholesome treatment of human relationships, one calling for mutual generosity of spirit. Duty, in this sense, calls first for acknowledgement of others' existence and recognition of the divine, even within the lowliest citizens of society. From this virtue's font shall flow respect and good order within families and societies. Without adherence to Duty, we need search no farther to discover the negative results of our neglect.

If there is hazard in approaching such a subject, it stems not from the definition of that four-letter word—d - u - t - y—and its implications for individual and societal freedom. Instead, strife occurs when individuals and governmental institutions lose sight of duty as a Christian virtue. Evil results from conversion of holy duty into a dark desire for power, authority, and domination of others. We witness this distortion when those in positions of power oppress the poorest, most fragile members of society.

In treading the unsteady terrain of

duty, I become aware of my own weakness and fallibility. May the Lord prevent me from writing as if every word I pen is divinely inspired. Any flaws, whether doctrinal or human, are my doing and no other's. I take full responsibility before God and you, my readers.

This treatise flows from an interior need to clarify for myself issues raised in the sacred writings of the New Testament on the subject of duty. Even when—if—God grants me the grace, strength, and authorial insight to complete this meditation, I realize that these words I pen may never take flight beyond the walls of our cathedral environs. They may never cross the boundaries of our diocese. It makes no difference. I share from my heart the voice I hear in the silence of intimate prayer. . . . "You are loved. You are blessed. Become what you pray."

The words of Psalm 71, verse 15 come to mind: "My lips shall proclaim your intervention and tell of your salvation all day, little though it is what I can understand."

Following the path of revelation, I shall speak to the duties of each one, from the most powerful in our midst to the neediest and most dependent among us.

In this way does St. Matthew speak of duty in Chapters six and seven of his Gospel. The evangelist lays out in the Lord's own words the human reality according to which each of us must live internally and behave toward others, according to our station in life.

I am, for example, a bishop of the Roman Catholic Church—albeit an obscure one, being as I am far removed from ecclesial and political seats of power. The very nature of this call to write and my acceptance of this sacred charge place obligations of duty and service on me, exceeding what is expected from others. Conversely, I am not bound by the duties of civic leaders charged with providing a safe environment for daily living. At its most basic level, each citizen must respect others' right to life and liberty.

I shall reflect in depth on teachings related to duty as found in Saint Paul's letters to his beloved communities in Ephesus, Corinth, and Rome (written in anticipation of his arrival there). We have much to learn about the Christian life by embracing the two Letters of Saint Peter in which he addresses spouses, parents, and young adults— servants, too. Finally, we shall profit from reviewing the Letter to the Hebrews and its wise expression of the meaning of true fidelity as followers of Jesus Christ, the Chosen People's true Messiah.

I have collated these injunctions into what I pray you will find a harmonious whole. I offer this work to you now as both a gift from God and a joyous labor of my own love for the people of God.

Jean Valjean, my brother, you no longer belong to evil, but to good. It is your soul that I buy from you; I withdraw it from black thoughts and the spirit of perdition, and I give it to God.

Fantine, Book the Second, Chapter XII,
The Bishop Works

When Jean Valjean left the Bishop's house, as we have seen, his mood was one that he had never known before. He could understand nothing of what was passing within him. He set himself stubbornly against the angelic deeds and the gentle words of the old man, "You have promised me to become an honest man. I am purchasing your soul, I withdraw it from the spirit of perversity, and I give it to God Almighty."

Fantine, Book the Second, Chapter XIII,
Petit Gervais

Foreword

Long before Jean Valjean knocked on my door, I had conceived the idea of writing a book about our Father-God, whom I love and serve, or better, serve because his love bestows and invites my love.

Apart from holding myself to the highest human standards, I demand nothing from anyone, excuse even the most egregious behavior, embrace with compassion the most despised sinner. In the oft-stated opinion of my sister,

Baptistine, I go too far in rewarding what she calls my "ungodly" behavior with "profligate" (her term, not mine) generosity (my term not hers).

Since my encounter with "that Valjean fellow," as Baptistine still refers to him, my desire to write has burst from a quivering taper into a now unquenchable flame. Most nights I repair to my quarters after supper and continue to ponder and write, even after Baptistine retires, along with our dear and faithful housekeeper, Madame Magloire.

I deem this solitary time a blessed gift. My daily "bishop work" has come to an end. The citizens of Digne have retired for the night, weary from the day's labor and difficulties. All sound within our humble residence ceases.

Most nights, I write till well past midnight. Or until my weary, watery eyes blur the lines of script on the page.

Though I am—nominally at least—master of this house, I scramble to bed for a few hours' sleep, avoiding thereby my sister's scolding clucks when I stifle a yawn during morning Mass. On those rare occasions of abundant inspiration, I remain at my table until dawn's first rays creep across the sill announcing the birth of a new day.

I often wonder, deep into those silent nights, while searching for the perfect word or turn of phrase, what became of my wild-looking parolee, my son and brother in Christ. Like King Melchisedek in Genesis 14, the formerly nameless prisoner 24601 appeared at my door, seemingly from nowhere and everywhere. At my invitation, he spent but a night beneath our roof. He reappeared the next morning in custody of two triumphant gendarmes but departed a free man, never to be heard from again.

The events of that memorable night and following morn—Baptistine's discovery of what she deemed a robbery, the parolee's second arrival as a thief in tow—everything surrounding that blessed encounter has remained with me, dare I say haunted me. Of one thing I am certain. Jean Valjean's unannounced appearance at my home and his unexpected reappearance provided the catalyst I needed to conceive this book. Within the context of that pivotal sequence of events, I intended to address the topic of Christian duty. Now, after too long a delay, I begin.

As an aside, I alone among that cast of characters outside my residence held out hope that a life of goodness might be ahead for this wretched, fate-abused man. To the women of my household, the gendarmes, and a cluster of curious neighbors gathered outside my door, Valjean seemed destined for a well-deserved return to the galleys, where he had already spent two decades minus a year before his recent parole.

I spoke to this bereft but beloved child of God words I had never spoken to any other in so direct a manner: "My son, I have purchased your soul for God, and you have promised me to use this silver to become an honest man." I felt in that instant that the beaten-down and condemned Christ had commandeered my spirit . . . and my voice.

Did any of it make a difference to

that despairing man? The Lord has not seen fit to let me know. Such is the ministry of a pastor. Christ appears in a different human form each day. In each encounter, I have one moment, out of the countless trillions allotted to me, to let Him speak through me barely one sentence before the moment passes into eternity. God help me if I fail to recognize that moment and respond as He would.

I never heard the name, Jean Valjean, again. Yet, he lives on within me. Over the years, I have fought mightily the temptation to speculate on what became of our once-treasured

Myriel heirlooms. Mine was only to commend that desperate, frightened man to our Father-God and to his son Jesus, the divine lover of all who are poor and suffering, his beloved "miserables."

Back to my topic.

Duty

As I experience and profess it, duty means far more than adherence to the "shalls" and "shall nots" of Holy Mother Church and the State. The sacred virtue of "doing one's duty" soars beyond obedience to regulations and laws, collected and added to over the course of eighteen centuries of Christian history. Daily, I commit to live the external and interior parts of my life each day by a simplified code my Brother Jesus taught me and everyone, each in our own eras, locales, and life circumstances:

"Love the Lord your God with all your heart, all your soul, all your strength, and all your mind. And, love your neighbor as yourself" — Luke 10:27.

That, my dear reader, is the very essence of Christian duty.

But who is my neighbor? In this, Jesus was quite clear. In response to the question posed to Him, Saint

Luke offers the parable of the Good Samaritan. Our neighbor is the "other," the one so easily despised. Our Savior left no doubt, no room for debate in Matthew's fifth chapter, the Beatitudes, and twenty-fifth chapter on justice. These core passages illustrate real-time examples for those tempted to qualify the Lord's meaning in practiced, self-serving excuses.

For this wise evangelist—formerly a despised tax collector—"duty" had nothing to do with force or fear of damnation or any sort of punishment, here on earth and in the great, mysterious hereafter. Rather, duty spoke to a higher call—to love with gratitude for blessings freely given, humbly received.

In that spirit, I now set out to record my convictions about the Christian call to duty.

Part the First

What time these various affairs and his devotions and his breviary left him, he gave first to the needy, the sick, and the afflicted; what time the afflicted, the sick, and the needy left him, he gave to labour. Sometimes he used a spade in his garden, and sometimes he read and wrote. He had but one name for these two kinds of labour; he called them gardening. "The spirit is a garden," said he.

Towards noon, when the weather was good, he would go out and walk in the fields, or in the city, often visiting the cottages and cabins. He would be seen plodding along, wrapt in his thoughts, his eyes bent down, resting upon his long cane, wearing his violet doublet, wadded so as to be very warm, violet stockings and heavy shoes, and his flat hat, from the three corners of which hung the three golden grains of spikenard.

His coming made a fete. One would have said that he dispersed his warmth and light as he passed along. Old people and children would come to their doors for the bishop as they would for the sun. He blessed and was blessed in return. Whoever was in need of anything was shown the way to his house. Now and then he would stop and talk to the little boys and girls—and give a smile to their mothers. When he had money, his visits were to the poor; when he had none, he visited the rich.

Fantine, Book the First, Chapter I,
An Upright Man

Chapter the First

Purity of Intention

This night, beyond my desk candle's flickering orb, there lurks in a shadowed corner of my bedroom a moment of icy dread. I can best describe it as blank-page paralysis. The silence of our home, my quill hovering inches above pregnant paper . . . they call me to sire words conceived mentally in daylight but held in abeyance until now. Scattered thoughts and elusive words, like pieces of a puzzle, demand assembly. They harbor no concern regarding my literary inexperience and the fragility of their own uncertain lives.

I first conceived this book while contemplating the great mysteries of my life . . . every life.

Why was I born?

Who am I? By that, I mean the naked man beneath the episcopal robes and high office.

What is my God-bestowed duty in this life? The purpose of my life, my *raison d'etre*? On this very day. In this fleeting moment.

How many years have I left? How few? I have already outlived many of my peers.

What beckons beyond the grave?

Any answers I claim to possess are those nurtured by decades of prayer, ministry, and personal suffering. They arose through strata of human experience and tested faith. This night . . . here at my desk . . . quill pen, ink and paper stand ready, trembling with the anticipation of a lover's arrival. I feel—how shall I describe it?—*impelled* . . . yes, the proper word. Decades-old personal sharings cry out for retrieval from private, dust-covered storage within my soul's inner chambers. Dare I dredge up long-buried, random memories from birth to yesterday and today? Can I? These are stored and remain in great part, at least, unavailable in the real time of a fleeting moment.

Heavenly Father, I pray for the grace of accurate retrieval.

Pressing on, I commit to stacking one word upon another until a sentence forms. May these word clusters evolve into paragraphs capturing concepts that dance and tease at the edges of my mind. I will strive for clarity of expression in the earthbound poverty of language and my own age-dulled imagination. Like a child on Christmas morning, I crave to open gifts yet concealed within the recesses of my untapped spirit. With faith in the Holy Spirit, my divine muse, I envision paragraphs collecting into a single chapter, then another, until the work signals its own conclusion.

In these moments, I understand how the elation of creative writing, idealized in the abstract, breaks down under the higher calling of self-preservation. Rather than expend my flagging energy and suffer sleepless nights, would it not be preferable to protect my interior life— my true Self—from exposure to the world, the possibility of ecclesiastical censorship and, worse, critical ridicule. There exists yet another more dangerous possibility than critical ridicule. Success. Fame. Notoriety.

These outcomes, I fear, would not serve my personal best interests or those of the good people God commissions me to serve. The prospect of these fragile pages outliving me raises another point of caution. Such a daunting prospect races steed-like through the crooked lanes of faulty memory of past events. Might future readers, be they admiring or hostile, judge the man, the priest, the bishop solely on this fallible published text?

I must decide whether to expose these pages to the outside world, setting loose the fruit of latenight binges to the glaring daylight of unknown readers. Can I trust strangers to parse correctly my meaning and intent?

Thoughts of aborting this project at conception tempt me, as the sweet, juicy apple enticed the first human couple into the greatest mistake of their lives. A mistake the effects of which I—all of us—suffer after eons of life hardscrabble earth.

Would I serve love better by leaving behind when I die nothing other than a leatherbound folder containing only blank pages?

On the other hand, might my surrender to doubt equate with partaking of the forbidden fruit? Perhaps I should add this codex to my last will and testament:

"Any and all pages written by my hand are to be destroyed upon my death."

Caught in this tug-of-war moment, I discern your voice, my Risen Savior, prompting, "Charles Francois, called by many Bienvenu, I deem the fruit of your life's experience and spiritual journey worthy of preservation for the instruction and edification of others *in perpetuum*."

Having received this affirmation from above, I hold fear in abeyance . . . and proceed. My focus—my guiding compass—shall be the gospels and letters of the New Testament. I pray, "Lord Jesus, show me the way forward into my treatise on the subject of Duty." In response, I sense the Spirit whispering, "The Sermon on the Mount." I recognize the gentle voice from another turning point in my life. On that occasion, it called me from untimely and despairing widowhood to service as priest of the Roman Catholic Church into which the waters of Baptism had claimed me as an infant.

And so I write, fully aware that this initial draft will surely demand revisions, as will each chapter one by one. From the outset, I shall approach this work *ad majorem Dei Gloria*, not for my own glory but His. I accept this inspiration as acquiescence to a divine invitation and resolve, I pray, "My Lord Jesus, let my first written words be in the service of your greater glory."

"Be careful not to make a show of
your righteousness before people. . . .
When you give something to the poor,
do not have it trumpeted before you. . .
. If you give something to the poor,
do not let your left hand know what
your right hand is doing, so that your

gift remains really secret. Your Father who sees what is kept secret, will reward you." —Matthew 6:1-4

Who understands better than you, my Risen Lord, the fragile line between virtue and vice in one's service to the poor? The secrecy you speak of cloaks a virtuous act, so that ego may disappear. Concealed virtue guards the gate of human acclaim, preserving purity of intention from contamination.

*　　*　　*

Three sentences. Already I feel spent, drained of inspiration. I move my pen toward its waiting well, unsure if I am able or even need to write another word. Ever. But my muse frees me, urges me on . . .

I have striven each day to walk that line with joy and spiritual sobriety, teetering neither left nor right. My daily concern is for the needs of the people I serve, not the privilege of my position. I have witnessed during my lifetime the dark shadows of violent societal upheaval. You call me to minister equally and alike to ardent, no-matter-what believers and to indifferent, disaffected nonbelievers, of whom there are many. My greatest challenge, Lord Jesus, is to reveal you anew and witness to you as the perpetual outcast—the one having "nowhere to lay his head" — Luke 9:58.

Rereading what I have just written, I jot a marginal note . . .

> Christ's body here on earth . . .
> wounded, scarred, like Jean
> Valjean's, but still alive.

A spirit of concern for others brought me to Digne and this cozy episcopal home. Now, with swirling late-night thoughts and too few words scratched on the page before me, I happily occupy this chair at my old desk in this ample room. I heed an insistent call to continue writing . . .

> Upon my arrival in Digne, I discovered the truth of that Body of Christ far distant from my Paris upbringing and equally far from Rome where God planted the seed of my vocation. I inherited a spacious episcopal residence, befitting—people

thought—my "high" ecclesial office.

Upon arrival, I found on the same property a smaller, ill-equipped building serving as Digne's only hospital for the poor. A heroic band of Sisters of Charity cared for the sick in a few rooms overflowing with patients.

Duty prompted—nagged at—me to a convert my episcopal "palace" into a facility more suitable for the numerous ill and dying. Appalled at the disparity, shamed by the imbalance, I chose to make the lesser building my home.

News of the exchange soon spread to the priests of my diocese, to Digne's mayor and the town council, all of whom expressed displeasure with their new bishop's decision. As if I—an outsider—had somehow besmirched my episcopal status and their reputation in the region. To be honest, this accusation stung me. But, as Pontius Pilate said about his ordered inscription on the sign nailed to the cross above Jesus' head, "What I have written, I have written" (John 19:22). I believed I could do no other than follow my Lord's mandate.

Again, in the service of truth, I confess to a lingering doubt. Had I gone too far in disturbing the status quo? Again, I received and still honor a divine whisper of approval. Shortly after completing the transfer, a prominent Monsignor of my diocese paid me a visit. When he began with, "Your Excellency," I prepared for a respectful scolding.

"Please, call me Father," I insisted, "for you and I share the one sacrament of Holy Orders, sprung from the priesthood of all the baptized." He acknowledged my reference to 1 Peter 2:9. "Father," he continued with obvious discomfort, "your decision about the episcopal residence. It has our people . . your people . . . wondering . . . talking."

"What exactly is the nature of their

. . . wondering?"

"A bishop has a certain . . . status . . . a . . . higher place and office among the clergy and civic authorities. They expect a certain . . . well, standard." "

As do I," I replied.

"Then you agree?" He looked upon me as would a professor having achieved a breakthrough with a stubborn student.

"Our standard is Christ and him alone. How could I live in luxury, Father, while the Sisters next door struggle to provide for our many patients in such a cramped, unhealthy environment? Would Jesus not have done the same?"

"Considering your decision in that way, Your Grace . . . Father, how can I not agree with your decision?" My triumph proved shortlived. Our conversation shifted to other, less divisive matters of diocesan business. Baptistine served tea and cakes, and the good pastor departed to report his failure to those who had delegated him to change their new prelate's mind.

I went to my room and knelt in prayer. "Lord Jesus, I learned from this visit that sometimes one cannot keep the left hand from knowing what the right is doing. Especially, when disagreement arises over which viewpoint is correct and which of the two is, shall I say, wellintended, even correct, but less so."

The people of Digne moved on, accepting that the Church had sent them a rather strange, but all-in-all harmless bishop. I pray that, over time, they have come to pride themselves on having the largest, best-equipped, and free hospital in the region.

I feel elated that my "grand opus" on the meaning of gospel Duty has at last begun. With my authorial insights nearly exhausted and my meager harvest safely secured in a desk drawer, I resolve to succumb to needed sleep.

Begging for a momentary delay, I ask the Lord's indulgence to add these few verses that have played at the back of my mind all evening:

Blank Pages

enter stage left
a barren stage
on which to pen
my life story
many pages needed
to flesh out
the passing years'
own true tales
with past penned
today needs telling
blank pages wait
author eager daunted

[Bishop Myriel] believed that faith is healthful. He sought to counsel and to calm the despairing man by pointing out to him the man of resignation, and to transform the grief which looks down into the grave by showing it the grief which looks up at the stars.

M. Myriel could be summoned at any hour to the bedside of the sick and dying. He did not ignore the fact that therein lay his greatest duty and his greatest labor. Widowed and orphaned families had no need to summon him; he came of his own accord. He understood how to sit down and hold his peace for long hours beside the man who had lost the wife of his love, of the mother who had lost her child. As he knew the moment for silence, he knew also the moment for speech.

Fantine, Book the First, Chapter IV,
Works Answering Words

Chapter the Second

Faith

On this silent night, candles flicker on my desk. A blank page beckons to consider the meaning of faith. "Oh," I ask the void, "who am I to speak with authority on this unfathomable mystery?" In the silence, I hear a faint, non-accusatory whisper, "It was you, Charles, who chose the topics in your outline." Recognizing the sweet voice of my Lord and Savior, I take up my quill pen and prepare in unfeigned humility to write—still with haunting reservation as to my fitness to do so with either skill or depth of spirit . . .

At dawn one morning, a messenger summoned me to the bedside of a dying man. I offered him and his loved ones the only gift a man of faith can . . . hope.

A hope nourished at the banquet of imagination. I say this not on any authority of my own but by the sacred word of Scripture found in the first verse of the opening chapter of the Letter to the Hebrews:

"Faith is the assurance of what we hope for, being certain of what we cannot see."

Implicit in these words is Death, that monosyllabic conclusion of every life form's material existence. We do not have faith in death. We have seen too much of it in our lifetime. Ample sepulchers remind us of loved ones lost and others unknown to us.

Afterlife. Now we are in the realm of personal belief and nonbelief.

Those three syllables enwrap within their nine letters the greatest mystery of all. Who does not wonder what happens in that decisive moment when spirit bids adieu to its earthly companion and soulmate on this shared journey we call Life? Whatever one imagines regarding his continued existence in—if I may coin a word "Afterdeath," or better, "Afterlife"—truth lies beyond the knowledge and experience of the living.

All that dying persons can control is their attitude about leaving this life behind and moving on to whatever might be next—if anything. For some, their last living breath yields to descent into the dank hole of a forever grave. Others pass with the unprovable expectation of "more."

A great temptation in death allows our misguided conceit to believe that our departure must cause the world to end for all and everything. "How can life on earth go on without me?" we reason. Such are the power and breadth of human ego.

I confess to toying with this blatant untruth and thank my God for gentle reminders that I am but one man, neither the first of my kind nor the last. I am still of importance, however, in God's mysterious design for humanity and the universe.

Believers in the promise of Afterlife release their hold on this life in the hopebased conviction of lifting their newfound life-sight to the outer reaches of the universe . . . and beyond. We do so, if I may, in "certain" <u>hope</u> that our life will continue, not end. We expect both a new place to call home and a new commission in our ongoing, eternal evolution.

Again, I reprise Jean Valjean—he is never far from my consciousness—and that moment when he pounded his fist on my door and begged entry and shelter. I recall every word he spoke in his crude but honest introduction. I made no conscious effort to engrave them on my memory, yet they remain for instant summons, all these decades after:

"See here. My name is Jean Valjean. I am a convict from the galleys. I have passed nineteen years in the galleys. I have been walking for four days since I left Toulon. I have travelled a dozen leagues today on foot. "This evening, when I arrived in these parts, I went to an inn, and they turned me out, because of my yellow passport, which I have shown at the town hall. I had to do it. I went to an inn. They said to me, 'Be off!' No one would take me.

"I went to the prison; the jailer would not admit me. I went into a dog's kennel; the dog bit me and chased me off, as though he had been a man. One would have said that he knew who I was. I went to the fields, intending to sleep in the open air, beneath the stars. There were no stars. I thought it was going to rain, and I reentered the town, to seek the recess of a doorway. Yonder, the square, I meant to sleep on a stone bench.

"A good woman pointed out your

house to me and said to me, 'Knock there!' I have knocked. What is this place? Do you keep an inn? I have money, savings—one hundred and nine francs fifteen sous—which I earned in the galleys by my labor in the course of nineteen years. I will pay. What is that to me? I have money. I am very weary; twelve leagues on foot; I am very hungry. Are you willing that I should remain?"

Never had I witnessed such despair, so much mental and Spiritual pain. Valjean had lost any faith he once might have had. He did not believe in a benevolent God. Nor had he faith in anyone living, least of all in himself. How could faith survive in one who found it impossible to grasp the thinnest thread of hope. Two decades of prison and slavery in the galleys had beaten out of him all that was good and decent, leaving behind an abandoned shell— perhaps better, a wild beast with a human soul. With any trace of hope forever out of reach, he imagined nothing loftier than a solitary life of suffering, ravenous hunger, and the kind of soul-deadening injustice he had endured for those seemingly eternal years.

I myself know not for certain what awaits me in the instant following my death. Nor does any human possess proof of what does or does not exist on the other side of that great chasm. Human existence on this planet is the only reality we know. Is death truly, as religious folk hold, a transfer point connecting one form of life and another? Or, is death a definitive end—a bridge to nowhere, so to speak?

Even as Christians, we base our descriptive conclusions on not seeing, on possessing no definitive proof beyond the promise made to the repentant sinner on the first Good Friday:

"This day you shall be with me in paradise."—Luke 23:43

My personal belief, based on the teachings of Jesus of Nazareth, as found in the New Testament, is that there is no such state of existence as "dead." The only enduring reality, once our mothers conceive and give birth to us, is life. Only the "form" of life shall change. I do acknowledge that highly intelligent men and women, each a scholar in his or her own right, are equally convinced that humans do not possess within their essence an immortal life force.

I base my conviction that life continues beyond death solely on faith, not knowledge. My personal decision for faith is rooted in two wonderful—yes, wonder-full—human resources, "hope" and "imagination." Hope stems from my grace-full understanding of humanness in this life as a union of immortal spirit and perishable matter.

Imagination allows me to "see in the dark."

The atheist's end of life conviction is likewise rooted in "not seeing." In the end, each of us is, oddly enough, a "believer." Despite the opining of wise seers and Christian theologians, there is no absolute proof for or against the existence of life after death.

With wisdom, enlightened by humility, Saint Paul the Apostle admitted the limitations of human knowledge in First Corinthians 13:12:

"At present we see indistinctly, as in a mirror. . . . At present, I know only partially."

In that darkness of unseeing, Paul surrenders to imagination-fired hope: "Then, I shall know fully, as I am fully known"

One word leaps from the page. "Then!"

Such a faith-filled proclamation of hopeful expectation in that singular word.

* * *

Recent history in France and my own life experience have exposed a peculiar trait in human nature. Expression of faith—whether religious or atheistic—easily surrenders to fear of the unknown. In my years of ministry to hearts and souls, the resulting state of "doubt" is often a prelude to a person's drawing close to the brink of radical conversion. This last phrase, "radical conversion," holds for the staunchest believer and the most militant unbeliever. Doubt can lead a believer to nonbelief; doubt can stir the heart of a nonbeliever to newfound faith.

A look into France's ancient and recent past dredges up images of fire and brimstone preachers of gospel "purity," whose own bleak interior lives betrayed what they professed. Spiritual blindness led them to demand perfection in others. Those deemed to have fallen short suffered the penalties of excommunication, damnation, and all too often horrific torture, even death. A terrible thing it is to demand orthodoxy, when one's own faith is lacking, even spiritually moribund. I think of battles fought on our own French soil between so-called Catholic armies of warring kings of France and England. Joan of Arc became an archetype of this injustice—sainted by one side, condemned by the other to burn as a heretic and witch. All in the name of Jesus Christ whose prime requirement was to love one another and forgive each other (John 13:34).

When love and forgiveness prevail in a soul, be it of a believer or nonbeliever, there is the Christ reincarnated and alive once more in our world.

As a young militant pharisee, Saul of Tarsus, epitomized this combative style of orthodoxy. At the height of his terrorizing campaign against Jewish followers of Jesus, he came to a spiritual crossroad. In a life-altering vision he encountered, in a form he could describe only as "light" and "spoken words" (seen and heard by himself alone, it seems), that same Jesus of Nazareth whose followers he swore to wipe from the face of the earth.

The vision-voice posed a simple question (Acts 9:4), "Saul, why are you doing this . . . to _me_?"

Terrified at the voice and blinded by searing light, Saul responded with a trembling but perfectly understandable question of his own. "Who are you?"

The very question any one of us would have asked, finding ourselves in his situation.

"I am Jesus . . . the one you persecute."

Driven by indignation and religious zeal, Paul had received his license to take prisoners, without possessing accurate information affirmed by deep introspection.

I recognize this same behavior in my own high minded, religiously indifferent youth. Political, social, and religious revolutions boiled in the same black kettle during my early adulthood, resulting in the peril of standing on the wrong side of social movements and political debate.

How? By way of my noble inheritance.
At the other end of the spectrum, I
have personally known freethinkers who
turned their lives around the moment
they allowed the light of their personal
"Damascus experience" to knock them
down. I believe that, even before Saul
's grace-filled moment of conversion, he
must have allowed himself to admit just
the barest possibility of having made the
wrong decision in choosing the orthodox
side of Jewish religious history and
theology. After all, had he not stood as
an approving witness to the stoning of
Stephen, the first Christian martyr.

On the way to Damascus, Saul
yielded to a benevolent life force greater

and more powerful than himself. When I encounter and listen to those who belittle religious belief, I ask myself, "Is it Christ Jesus you reject? Or, is your rebellion against the way our Catholic Church's priests and we, the hierarchy, misrepresent and poorly model the true Christ?"

What is my solemn duty, then, as a man of faith, a priest, now bishop? In response, I hear the crystal voice of the Spirit: "Never lose your craving for wisdom, deeper faith, and loving commitment to serving the poor in the midst of social unrest and political upheaval." With your help, Dear Lord. With your help.

Credo

yes to unseen
unproven conviction
fist to breast pressed
blotting inner
outer denial

trust feeble intuition
always yes when
no rules the day
makes more sense
in the moment

credo not today
or tomorrow solely
in tight spots
yes in doubt
with all awry

to the divine
but gift of unseen
faith's not mine
my work my gift
one who shares

earth cannot bind
faith gives wings
to realms unseen
mysteries given light
. . . because i believe

When [Bishop Myriel] talked with that infantile gaiety that was one of his graces . . . all felt at ease in his presence, and from his whole person joy seemed to radiate. His ruddy and fresh complexion, and his white teeth all of which were well preserved, and which he showed when he laughed, gave him that open and easy air which makes us say of a man: he is a good fellow; and of an old man: he is a good man.

Fantine, Book the First, Chapter XIII,
What He Believed

Chapter the Third

Elusive Joy

On a sunny Roman day, made for music, dance and romance, I abandoned what little faith I claimed. Kneeling beside my beloved's fresh-dug grave, I begged whatever fates might listen, "Take me with her."

Never again, I thought, would I experience the joy I discovered on our wedding day. If there ever was such a benevolent being as God, he or it had abandoned me on foreign soil with no one and nothing remaining to live for. In that moment of grieving blindness, I had no foresight of divine surprises lying in my path, soon to restore my belief in the possibility of joy in this life.

I endeavor this night to put in writing for the first time that ever available gift. Where better to begin than with the word itself?

Joy
Another of those human states of being

so easy to experience in the moment and describe in its aftermath. In the second chapter of Saint Luke's Gospel, verses 10-11, joy is an angel's proclamation to rough-and-tumble shepherds as they watched over their sheep during the night that Jesus, our Lord and Savior, was born.

"Do not be afraid; I am here to give you good news, great joy for all the people. Today, a Savior has been born to you in David's town; he is the Messiah and the Lord."—Luke 2:8-20

How could they not have responded with terror of this once-in-a-lifetime phenomenon? To their credit, the shepherds' curiosity overcame reluctance to believe their alarming visitors, who vanished with all the suddenness of their arrival.

As I walk the lanes and alleyways of my off-the-path episcopal town of Digne, I am sad to say I encounter little joy. Oh, yes, there are smiles on the faces of my fellow citizens of all ages, both the rich and the poor. I wonder, are their smiles and laughter indicative of deep-seated contentment which, over the years, I have come to associate with joy? I do fear that in many cases I would not answer in the affirmative. Smiles and laughter do not equate with a state of internal, indelible joy.

So, what is this virtuous state we call Joy? How to recognize it? In ourselves? In others? Even more important, how does one snare it from an atmosphere for the most part shrouded in spiritual darkness and numbing societal despair?

I can only speak for myself, from my personal life experience. As a child, I grew toward manhood under the strict supervision of a demanding father and a mother who supported his demands for my education and comportment, conforming to the station of my birth. Only when alone with me did Mother show her tender side, giving witness to another, less rigid option for human comportment.

As a young student, what I called "joy" was a fickle, fleeting state of mind, present one day, nowhere to be found the next. I enjoyed the company of my fellow students, especially our shared laughter at a juicy, off-color story. Likewise, I relished our highminded philosophical discussions during which, among ourselves at least, we solved—in the abstract, of course—the great social and political issues and conflicts of our time.

Upon conclusion of my formal education, I consented to marriage with a pleasing young woman, who proved to be both a compatible and affectionate partner. With her I discovered a level of happiness previously beyond my reach, even beyond my comprehension. Looking back on my life, I now admit that my contentment rested, in large part, on the circumstances of my privileged life, not on any deep-seated sense of wholeness within myself, certainly not with God. At that time, the deity I occasionally prayed to sprang from the cultural milieu of my upbringing. Faith existed, at best, on the fringes of my daily consciousness.

When flames of revolt showed signs of licking at the boots of people of my class and position, Father decided that I should take my bride to a place of safety beyond the borders of France. We journeyed south far across the Alps, all the way to Rome. We settled there with the intention of raising a family and living in peace, until it might be safe to return home and resume our rightful place among the elite of French society.

Was I happy in exile? These two concepts . . . "happy" and "exile" seem contradictory. Reviewing that period of my life, especially as months became years, I find it more and more difficult to attach to it the concept of Joy.

A related word, "contentment," more accurately describes my state of being. Selfishly, I was glad to be away from the turmoil that had overtaken French society. My heart ached at separation from family and companions, everything familiar which I expected to be my permanent state of being.

I found great solace in the companionship of my dear wife. I cherished our time together, our lovemaking on steamy Roman nights when the air was still and stagnant. Being in love allowed us to survive the loss of what we left behind. The strangeness of adapting to a new people, unaccustomed food, and a new language grew easier over time. But, Joy? I cannot attach that unique label even to that Camelot period of my life.

If there was any hope of discovering a deeper state of Joy in our new surroundings, my wife's lingering illness and subsequent death removed all hope of it, seemingly for the remainder of my life. How could I predict a second chance at life and the dawning of that elusive state would ever be mine in this life? Yet, from the ash heap of solitary grief and despair, Joy sprang to life.

How did this occur? I cannot speak for any other person, since divine grace is made to order for each of us and delivered to our doorstep at just the right moment. This is my story of finding true Joy. It rose from the grey ash of widowhood. (I confess it still pains me to pen that dreaded word.)

Let me begin by affirming a long-held conviction. I do not believe God directly willed my beloved to be taken from me so early in our wedded life and so far from home, as a kind of trial or punishment.

May I offer a feeble, middle ground theological position on this? I am confident in attributing my life circumstances to God's broader plan for my place in this great universe we call "creation." I needed to be stripped of everything I held dear—spouse, family, native country, even for a time the language of my birth.

Standing spiritually naked before myself and the Lord, I experienced a new (how can I describe it?) "lightness of being." To put it another way, I encountered for the first time since my beloved's death—and to my great surprise—the gift of . . . Joy.

I don't recall making a conscious decision about what happened next. I can only say I found myself kneeling in a pew at the beautiful and stately church of Santa Francesca Romana. I knew nothing about the woman whose essence permeated this church in which I prayed that day. I later learned that her life straddled the fourteenth and fifteenth centuries. Being a devoted wife and mother, she nursed her husband through the last seven years of his life. Our stories ran parallel in that respect. Following his death, Francesca entered a Benedictine monastery and devoted herself to prayer and charitable works among Rome's most impoverished citizens. I had no intention of following her along that path.

I consider it more than a coincidence, rather the Holy Spirit's guidance, that I had stumbled into a massive church named after a sainted woman who had lived my life and, further, to find that we both had nursed a spouse through illness and subsequent death.

As I walked home that sunny morning, I spoke to Jesus in a manner I rarely, if ever, had—man to man. I asked what my future held? Was I meant to enter a monastery devoting my life to charitable works, like Francesca?

Although no clear answer came, I sensed I was . . . different . . . in a strange and wonderful way.

I experienced Joy for the first time in my life, without understanding why.

Joy

risen lord

the wasted time

energy sapping years

forfeited creativity

serving the charlatan

doom's town crier

years wasted

lost forever

indelible scars
upon the soul
beyond healing
no second chances
joy unsought
a staged mirage
not for me
not in this life
blood and fate
rejected at birth
mirage became real
a welcome stranger
bearing priceless gift
not silver plates
nor heirloom candles
but newfound Joy

Ongoing dialog with God was the source and lifeblood of Bishop Myriel's spiritual life. In the bishop's silent hours, Victor Hugo wrote:

"He contemplated the grandeur and the presence of God."

Fantine, Book the First,
Chapter XIII,
What He Believed

Chapter the Fourth

Our Need to Pray — Our Duty to Pray

Part 1

I recognize a potential hazard in writing a book that unknown others might take up. The reader may expect to find in my human words a deeper wisdom than I possess. Only they and God know their lives, their faith. I hear the Spirit calling me to pause . . . to reflect, before I scratch another sentence upon the page. . . .

Now, let me resume by calling upon that same Spirit to guide my quill pen along each line and through each subsequent page.

A young priest of my diocese asked me once if I prayed a great deal. I was sure he observed my perplexed look. After a moment's reflection, I replied with a soft, "Not a great deal. . . ." He looked startled—betrayed even—so I quickly followed with a second thought affirmation. ". . . but always."

He exhaled a delayed breath, seeming relieved and validated. I felt humbled and a bit frightened that my inadequate example should mean so much to him—for better or worse. My personal behavior and practice should neither affirm nor negate another's relationship with our Lord Jesus Christ. But, clearly it does. How could I have forgotten this?

Even at my age, a childlike wonder at life in all its forms still pervades my spirit. The source of that awe is expansive and full of surprises . . . a Father-God encompassing within the creative embrace every living and inanimate thing, seen and unseen, on earth, in the heavens . . . even beyond the beyond.

I compare God to my own experience as a husband in love with the "other half of his own heart"—like the breathtaking devotion I experienced firsthand during my too-few years of marriage. I make no effort to erase my past or withhold my rather late vocation. Expressing my understanding of divinity in terms of marital love, whether from the pulpit or in conversation with fellow clerics, has led some to suspect my "orthodoxy" and the quality of my Roman seminary education. Or, they even question—.among themselves, I hear, but never to my face—my fidelity to celibacy Aware of this judgment, yet confident in my assessment of the divine will.

I search for evidence of Father-God in the same sort of people and places in which Jesus encountered traces of divinity. Our Savior lived among the poor, whom he embraced as brothers, sisters, children of God, those disregarded for supposed sins, outcasts too, and all whom society marginalizes. Jesus reassured those whom his native Jewish society declared unclean that Yahweh had already and forever declared everything issuing from the Creator to be then and forever . . . "very good" (Genesis 1). This despite appearances and the walls most cultures erect to divide the children of God into rigid classes— the material and spiritual haves and have nots of this world.

Even the so-called lesser beings of the animal world gain my friendship and pity. I recall the day a large, hairy garden spider crossed my path in the garden behind our residence. The sight of his—or her?—speckled back, featuring what appeared to be a cruciform marking, filled me with a strange sense of joy born of compassion. This creature of God, carrying his daily cross, lacked the natural beauty of, say, a lovely rose. Few, if any, would pause in awe of its transcendent splendor—or even take notice of his bearing the cross of Jesus. "Poor thing," I assured the spider, "don't mind what people say about you. In you I have a reminder of the price paid long ago for my salvation. You are beautiful in my eyes. Even more so in the eyes of Creator-God who made you."

Duty, in my personal, limited understanding of the spiritual world, means more than adherence to the "shalls" and "shall nots" of, the biblical Ten Commandments and my own Church's voluminous canon laws I spent too much of my study time memorizing.

Duty soars well beyond obedience to ecclesial regulations collected and added to over nearly two millennia of Christian history. I do my best to live by Jesus' simplified code of unreserved love for God, service to my neighbor, respect for myself.

Duty, in its deepest meaning and practice, soars beyond command. To say this another way, I pray, not because I must but because my prayer derives from an ache in my soul for connection with the Divine Trinity from whom I sprang.

I can no longer do anything but pray—day and night, waking and sleeping, working and taking meals. Nothing good can happen in me or to me—or anyone else—without frequent (dare I say, constant) communication with the Source of all goodness and light.

I find daunting this endeavor to put my most intimate thoughts and convictions on the written page. There are nights when I stare . . . and stare . . . at a blank sheet. How can I know that what I write on any subject is my final word, *the* final word? Will I not see life differently at some future date? Perhaps next month? Must what I write here stand forever as my final word on that subject? I pray not. Does not the very act of putting one's inked pen to paper signal those words' future demise?

My appreciation for authors who dare to publish what they have written grows each night that I repair to my private space intent upon committing my bared soul to paper. I now find it easy to imagine the repressed desire of authors to stop the printing press, crying out, "Hold! I thought of something else I should have added"—or should have said differently . . . or screams to heaven for erasure. Tonight, another verse craves birth before I sleep.

The Simple Path

religions tend to

complicate salvation

do it this way

avoid that or else

closing doors flung

wide upon the cross

by what right do
we deny the crucified
his dying appeal
forgive them
they know not
what they do

When you pray, do not use a lot of words, as the pagans do, for they hold that the more they say, the more chance they have of being heard. Do not be like them. Your Father knows what you need, even before you ask him. This, then, is how you should pray: "Our Father in heaven. . . ."
Matthew 6:7-9

Chapter the Fifth

Our Need to Pray—Our Duty to Pray

Part 2

I ask myself, "From whence do I receive encouragement and inspiration to continue my priestly ministry among my mostly peasant flock, in this forgotten corner of southeastern France?" Perseverance in ministry comes *from* prayer, *in* prayer, and *through* prayer. Without daily, hourly, moment-to-moment openness to the whisperings and promptings of the Spirit, I could not go on. In prayer, I bring my discouragement and any lurking self-doubt home to a Father eager to enfold me in His life-affirming embrace.

On this night that same love moves me to again take up my quill.

I wrote in Prayer, Part 1, the term, "duty," in relation to prayer is misleading in the current use of our mother tongue. It conveys one-sided obligation, but our heavenly Father neither demands nor requires us to pray as a condition of divine love and mercy.

We do well to parse with grace and care those few letters of the alphabet, d – u – t - y. Our goal is to mine a more subtle (mystical) understanding of this concept. What does it mean to say a child has a duty or obligation to love, respect, and obey a parent?

In our current 19th century mindset, Duty—especially within Roman Catholic teaching and practice—evokes the parenting style my contemporaries and I grew up with. I dare say it prevails to this day. This mandate expresses a relationship. One gone horribly awry at "loving God and failed humanity" from the dawn of our race's creation.

Thankfully, Christian spirituality and, I must assume, other forms of worship—even pagan—down through the ages always and everywhere sired extraordinary holy ones in their midst. There must exist, even now, someone in France whose clear-minded insight will force us to strive for an awareness of Duty based on a deeper comprehension of the nature of God. Or, colloquially, the "kind of God we have."

The sayings and parable stories of Jesus stand upon the firm foundation of Jewish faith, practice, and mysticism before his coming nearly two millennia past. Reading our inherited Scriptures with a faithful eye and open heart leads to a more accessible mystery of our relationship with divinity. The effect? An enlightened awareness of our God's benevolence.

A keystone of this renewed understanding is the parable of the loving father and his two quite opposite sons in that wonderful fifteenth chapter of St. Luke's gospel. Almost everyone, whether of deep religious faith or none, knows at least the basic outline of the "Prodigal Son" story. It should be noted that the Divine Storyteller himself gave no name or title to His fable. The common title is the invention of later scribes and partitioners of the sacred text.

For centuries, scholars have interpreted Jesus' story from the viewpoint of the younger, wastrel son who demanded his portion of the inheritance while his father still lived. The younger son peered into his own future and saw no future following the agrarian life of his dominant older brother, the "good" son.

Though hurt and dispirited, the young man's father granted his wish.

After packing his belongings, he left home with money in his pocket. He proceeded, through a lifestyle involving unwise, regrettable decisions, to squander his money in gambling halls and the fleshpots of loose living.

When the son had finally emptied his pocket of the last shekel in his possession, his false friends abandoned him. No longer could he purchase what he needed to maintain his former status. Feeling impoverished and bereft for the first time in his life, he recalled the lifestyle enjoyed even by his father's servants. Compared to his current disgusting employment, slopping hogs, returning home in shame appeared the more attractive option. I suspect that, Jesus' audience had shifted their focus to the entertaining sins of the younger son and his halfhearted, self-serving penitential resolve. Yes, Jesus went on, that young man acknowledged his unworthiness for full readmission into the family he betrayed.

Who among us, beginning with myself, cannot discover at least a trace of our own selves in this benighted young man?

As my own understanding of our good and loving God evolves (through the passage of many decades and the graying of thinning hair), I begin to view this story with new insight. Who is the real protagonist of the story? Not the foolish son. Not his pouting elder brother. It is the loving father himself. His unconditional love for both sons never wavered, despite his wounded heart.

Jesus describes this suffering man's daily routine. As the late afternoon sun dipped to the horizon at the end of each workday, the father walked to his estate's highest hill. From there he gazed down the road as far as sight allowed.

This he did for several years, it seems. In all that time, during countless sleepless nights, that loving father never lost hope that, in the haze of an evening's twilight, he would espy the figure of his returning son.

Would it be in halfhearted shame or with a truly repentant heart? He dared not predict.

The hoped-for day arrived!

"Father, I have sinned against Heaven and before you. I no longer deserve to be called your son," came the penitential confession (Luke 15:21). Yes, he fell into his father's arms with his rehearsed apology and proforma willingness to take a lower place "among the hired workers."

I worry that Jesus' listeners failed to grasp the deeper moral for themselves.

Nor did subsequent generations of Christians, it appears. Do we? Do I? For centuries, we have clucked our tongues at the younger son's cheekiness and debauchery, his insincere confession. But, Jesus' message (moral) hardly focused on the younger son.

In truth, the main protagonist of this timeless drama is that loving father himself. The boy expected a righteous, "How dare you?" and "Have you no comprehension of the bottomless suffering you caused me? And not just me but your entire family."

We hear none of that! The good, longsuffering man held no room in his heart for blame or reprisal. Instead, instant reconciliation with the bedraggled creature and a 'welcome home' feast (after, I presume, a badly needed bath and change of clothing from our bin of donated garments). Jesus' implicit message for all of us in this story is: "Note well, my children. That loving father represents exactly the kind of God you have in heaven."

I confess my personal return to my heavenly Father took a circuitous path and many years. In that time, I experienced marriage to a bride—not of my choice but, surprisingly, of my heart. Then, political exile from my homeland.

Followed by the pain of losing my beloved spouse in the prime of her vivacious young life.

My Lord capped my unexpected reconversion to the neglected faith of my Baptism with an unforeseen (miraculous!) call to priesthood. Yes, it took this stirring of the pot of joy and suffering in my life for me to grasp the deeper significance of St. Luke's oft-repeated family drama.

By the grace of God, I gained— albeit late—clear insight, an enlightened understanding of this amazing parable with which Jesus gifted us. The affixed title, "Parable of the Prodigal Son," had misled me—and Christians of all denominations. In truth, if the Divine Storyteller had assigned a title, it would have been "The Parable of the Loving Father."

Identification with the biblical father and my dawning understanding that our God is all-loving enabled me to open my residence door to every presumed prodigal who comes to me, including Jean Valjean. Without question, we made room at our table for that bedraggled beggar, laid out—as always—our family's heirloom silver, provided a clean, comfortable bed for the night. I surmised it to be the first soft mattress Valjean had seen or lain on in many years.

When the police dragged the arrested "thief" back to my doorstep, how could I respond in any other way than that of the parable's loving father. After what may seem a meandering intrusion, we return to the appropriateness—or not—of calling prayer a duty (in the sense of binding obligation). The Old French word, "preiere," derives from the Latin "precarius," meaning "obtained by entreaty." These legalistic terms retreat in shame before prayer's true name: Gratitude.

Knowing that our God, like the father in the parable, loves me, yes even me, and you, no matter how or how often our human failure muddies the field of our relationship. To pray out of duty alone—sans intimate relationship—can only end in boredom, even guilt when we neglect prayer or conclude that our most fervent prayers seem met by indifferent silence from on high.

Prayer rooted in gratitude energizes both body and spirit. Charged with this new life force, prayer shouts "No" to duty, "Nonsense" to obligation, and a booming "Yes!" to Joy! Yes, to the excitement of encounter with our gentle, welcoming Father. This form of prayer opens our hearts to model our lives on the real Jesus of Nazareth.

The fruit of joyful prayer is the desire and commitment to welcome strangers, forgive injuries, and hope for what otherwise might seem hopeless.

In truth and with deep gratitude to the Indwelling Spirit, I have arrived at a point in my life where I can humbly witness before all I meet, "I pray, because in it I find a secure path to the essence of divinity."

It is my fervent prayer and greatest desire that you too, dear reader, are close to this same realization.

I cannot think clearly, even one more minute. Creeping exhaustion warns me that I need to close my eyes. So, enough writing for this night, lest I bear the wrath of my dear sister, who watches me at Mass and scolds me, should I yawn even once. Tomorrow, perhaps, or later I shall add a poem to this complete this chapter.

Like all old men, and like the majority of thinkers, he slept little. This brief slumber was profound. In the morning, he meditated for an hour, then he said his Mass, either at the cathedral or in his own house. His Mass said, he broke his fast on rye bread dipped in the milk of his own cows. He then set to work.

He visited the poor so long as he had any money; when he no longer had any, he visited the rich. As he made his cassocks last a long while, and did not wish to have it noticed, he never went out in town without his wadded purple cloak. This inconvenienced him somewhat in summer.

On his return, he dined. The dinner resembled his breakfast. At half-past eight in the evening he supped with his sister, (with) Madame Magloire, standing behind them and serving them at table. Nothing could be more frugal than this repast. . . . His ordinary diet consisted of vegetables boiled in water, and oil soup.

Fantine, Book the First, Chapter V,
How Monseigneur Bienvenu Made
His Cassock Last So Long

Chapter the Sixth

Fasting

Within the pages of my well-worn Bible lies the meaning of my life. An example is the bookmark I keep at Deuteronomy 30:19. In that ancient Hebrew text, Yahweh presents Moses with the most fundamental— and still applicable—of all human decisions: "I have set before you life and death, blessing and curse." In the event that someone should harbor doubt, Yahweh breathes a prompting, *Psstt, "Choose life!"*

Choices.

The moment I awaken, they tussle for attention.

So, why get up? Why face the labor of plowing that overgrown field? I confess to mornings, in the winter especially, when human instinct shrinks, like even the bravest soldier, from facing another day of battle. Negativity creeps into my soul on mornings whose prospects offer dreary sameness or ill health (or both).

Aha! Such fears reveal exactly what I must write on the theme of fasting. Too great a leap? I pray not. We shall see.

At the heart of each life choice, opposites stand firm, eager for a struggle—be it or life or death. We make choices every day and move forward, either in their joy or under the weight of their burden. In the course of a single day, our fickle humanness pulls us this way . . . and that. Nonetheless, room exists for only one choice at a time.

Over the decades of my life, I have come to understand that surrender of the not-chosen unveils fasting's true meaning—letting go, even of something quite appealing. Our generous God sets the table for us.

Life

Death

Blessing

Curse

That same gracious grantor of human freedom will not choose for us.

Only a whispered, "Choose life,"

(Deuteronomy 30:19).

Some religious and philosophical disciplines place great emphasis on "letting go" based primarily on abstinence from food. Do I speak of my own local Church? What sense is that to the majority of people in my diocese, who fast yearround, living as they do, some in abject poverty, others at its unsecured border? Yet, the call to "fast" is universal. It invites rich and poor alike to acknowledge both their innate goodness and their periodic drift from sound decision making and right living.

That ancient dialogue between Yahweh and Moses, preserved in the Pentateuch, sheds light upon the true meaning of fasting. Following an unexpected divine call to leadership, Moses, having fled Egypt after murdering a cruel Egyptian slave master, now obeys Yahweh's shocking and personally risky call to return home and lead the oppressed Hebrew slaves to freedom across the Red Sea and through the blazing Sinai. To survive the barren wilderness, they searched each day for its insufficient edible gifts.

Acknowledging their complaints, Yahweh provided a food source the people referred to as "manna," which in their language meant "a substance exuded by the tamarisk tree."

"The Lord said to Moses: I am going to rain down bread from heaven for you. Each day the people are to go out and gather their daily portion."

Exodus 16:4

What was this food source? Edible plant excretions? Miraculous edible deposits? A mysterious edible something they could only describe as nature's nightly gift they awoke to at sunrise.

Such biblical parsing is beyond my scriptural training and failing memory. I must stay on point, lest I stray off the path.

It did not take long for the former slaves to grow bored with Yahweh's now-monotonous bounty. Yet, who could deny its life-sustaining benefit? Could anyone convince those near-starving wanderers that the holy way to penitential living lay in fasting from a food not of their choice?

Most good people of my diocese survive with similarly monotonous "manna" comprising their daily fare.

In urging his straggling wanderers to "choose life," Yahweh intended a kind of internal—spiritual—surrender, no longer to their former slave masters. Rather, to their God who is leading them to the very freedom they had dreamed of for decades. It had little to do with the formulaic penances mandated by later Jewish and Christian fasts. As always, Yahweh offered His simple but eminently challenging formula.

Nothing in the divine plan spoke of social class or financial capacity. The choice to live costs nothing in terms of tangible treasure yet demands what is still a fearsome price for us in the 19th century. To personalize this lesson, I need only to remind myself of the jagged path of my life, first as obedient son, then husband-nurse, and later—who could have predicted?—as priest, then bishop of the same Roman Catholic Church to which I had formerly paid meager lip service.

During those early, sunsplashed years abroad, I was by no means a man of prayer. During the sunny years of our marriage, my love and desire for

the woman who braved sharing life with
this selfcentered aristocrat sustained me.
I wanted nothing more. I needed
nothing more . . . so I thought.

These memories warm my heart on cold nights.
Only to the grantor of that carnal-spiritual gift dare I
admit how much I cherished my beloved. In the
hiddenness of God's grace, and solely by His favor, I
experienced in my early manhood the greatest of all
forms of prayer—wholehearted love for another.

How rapidly that golden age yielded to my life's
most dreadful period. I miss her still and anticipate our
reunion in the life to come. With whom else but my
Lord and Savior Jesus the Christ can I share this part of
my life? Not Baptistine. Surely not with my fellow
clergy or the people we serve. Years of prayer and
contemplation—those spiritual twins—have nurtured
this harmonious insight into my seemingly separate life
stories. It is time to put these prayer-purchased insights
in writing.

Love stretches us beyond the perceived limits of conditional quid pro quo: "If you do (___fill in___) for me, I shall do (___fill in___) for you." The human heart has so much greater capacity for love than any narrow, narcissistic "if you" / "I will" formula. invites those consumed in its sustaining flame to expand their circle of inclusion, to cast love's net beyond

Love invites those consumed in its sustaining flame to expand their circle of inclusion, to cast love's net beyond its perceived capacity for just "we two." To paraphrase Jesus in Matthew 5:46, if we extend our hearts in love only to those whom we find attractive, what good is that? Love calls us to identify those we might otherwise avoid, whose presence—perhaps existence even—we would rather do without.

The decision to love opens us to share our time and talent—our very selves. Is time our most prized possession? Letting go of—yes, "fasting from"—personal time is of one human nature's most difficult challenges. Jealousy of time shrinks our presence on this planet and worse, our availability to our fellow humans in need. No individual suffers that temptation alone. Balancing the need for treasured personal space with the pressing needs of partner, children, and society is the ongoing struggle of every man and woman of good will. God knows well how I experience that warfare in my daily episcopal ministry.

I am prompted by my muse to jot a few lines on this theme. Should I violate my reticence to expose my poetic efforts? I shall allow it for now. A future draft may witness its demise.

Love Emeritus

i love you
how the words flow
across the tongue

glib but tired
half-true habits
soundless noise
unmeant unheard
instinct-blocked
from other's heart
what eager understudy
waits in wings
of romance—
love's more genuine self
what if
what if instead
i said,
i cherish you
ahh, cherish . . .
to hold another dear

take care of
protect and foster
cherish means all-in
naught in safe reserve
cupid's sharpest arrow
costing the lover
delighting the beloved
cherish
now there's love's
worthy sub

Listening

The daily option for life over death found in Deuteronomy 30:19 reveals Yahweh's second point of light: our fasting is, above all, a call to "listen."

Paying attention to a brother or sister requires setting aside our flawed insistence that no one can impart to us anything we do not already know.

Choosing life through listening wages combat against our need to be right—to be *proved* right—to win, as in combat against an enemy. Human encounters, wherein two mouths speak, no ears listen, wage war to exhaustion or death, or until one party or the other simply abandons the field, self-declaring unilateral victory. The victor then gloats in bitter (albeit empty and lonely) triumph.

We do well to listen to the cautionary tale of our Savior about the swept, clean, and empty house reinhabited by previously evicted evil spirits:

"When an impure spirit comes out of a person, it goes through arid places seeking rest and does not find it. Then it says, 'I will return to the house I left.' When it arrives, it finds the house unoccupied, swept clean and put in order. Then, it goes and takes with it seven other spirits more wicked than itself, and they go in and live

There. And the final condition of that person is worse than the first. That is how it will be with this wicked generation."
Matthew 12:43-45, also Luke 11:26

True conversation is a two-way exchange, a dialog. The "fasting of listening" demands respect for the other's opinions, feelings, and needs. It includes acceptance of differing styles and ways of problem solving.

The fasting involved in listening may cast light on a dark area of one's inner Self. This form of austerity begs us to "keep an open mind." In that way, and that alone, do we open ourselves to learn something—anything. In that way alone do we hear the voice of God speaking to and within the depth of our hearts.

Being One With

A third form of choosing life called for in Deuteronomy is letting go of all excuses keeping us from deeper union with our God, the source and purpose of existence. In our daily lives, this aspect of listening calls us to reject whatever separates us from those who deserve and need our daily love and close attention.

The fasting of being one with

challenges us to seek solidarity with our Lord in life's various manifestations and stages from birth to death. This applies to our need for compassionate identification—suffering <u>with</u> those who physically suffer or experience dire emotional need. One need only recall Matthew 8, the Beatitudes, "Blessed are . . ." and the storied description of the Last Judgment in Matthew 25: "I was . . . and you gave me. . . ."

The ship of my energy left port around ten p.m. and has now sailed far beyond midnight. Time to powder the ink on these final words: "I was . . . and you gave me. . . ." I must satisfy myself with having filled at least a few more pages in this first draft. I am ever grateful to my

Lord and Savior who never tires of "being one" with this unworthy minister of his Gospel. Good thing. Careful not to scatter hot wax from the flickering candles, I purse my lips and blow softly. Now half their original stature, these candles speak to how long I must have lost myself in this reflection on three of fasting's multiple facets. With little time remaining before the morrow beckons, I rest my quill in its well. The hour has come to remove my Roman collar and soutane, utter a prayer of gratitude, and snuff the flame on this productive night.

(A) large chest was brought and deposited in the presbytery for the Bishop by two unknown horsemen, who departed on the instant. The chest was opened; it contained a cope of cloth of gold, a miter ornamented with diamonds, an archbishop's cross, a magnificent crosier—all the pontifical vestments which had been stolen a month previously from the treasury of Notre Dame d'Embrun. In the chest was a paper, on which these words were written, "From Cravatte to Monseigneur Bienvenu."

"Did not I say that things would come right of themselves?" said the Bishop. Then he added, with a smile, "To him who contents himself with the surplice of a curate, God sends the cope of an archbishop."

"Monseigneur," murmured the cure, throwing back his head with a smile. "God—or the Devil."

The Bishop looked steadily at the cure, and repeated with authority, "God!"

When he returned to Chastelar, the people came out to stare at him as at a curiosity, all along the road. At the priest's house in Chastelar he rejoined Mademoiselle Baptistine and Madame Magloire, who were waiting for him, and he said to his sister: "Well!

was I in the right? The poor priest went to his poor mountaineers with empty hands, and he returns from them with his hands full. I set out bearing only my faith in God; I have brought back the treasure of a cathedral."

That evening, before he went to bed, he said again: "Let us never fear robbers nor murderers. Those are dangers from without, petty dangers. Let us fear ourselves. Prejudices are the real robbers; vices are the real murderers. The great dangers lie within ourselves. What matters it what threatens our head or our purse! Let us think only of that which threatens our soul."

Then, turning to his sister: "Sister, never a precaution on the part of the priest, against his fellow man. That which his fellow does, God permits. Let us confine ourselves to prayer, when we think that a danger is approaching us. Let us pray, not for ourselves, but that our brother may not fall into sin on our account."

However, such incidents were rare in his life. We relate those of which we know; but generally he *passed his life in doing the same things at the same moment. One month of his year resembled one hour of his day.*

As to what became of "the treasure" of the cathedral of Embrun, we should be embarrassed by any inquiry in that direction. It consisted of very handsome things, very tempting things, and things which were very well adapted to be stolen for the benefit of the unfortunate. Stolen they had already been elsewhere. Half of the adventure was completed; it only remained to impart a new direction to the theft, and to cause it to take a short trip in the direction of the poor. However, we make no assertions on this point. Only, a rather obscure note was found among the Bishop's papers, which may bear some relation to this matter, and which is couched in these terms, "The question is, to decide whether this should be turned over to the cathedral or to the hospital."

Fantine, Book the First, Chapter VII, Cravatte

Chapter the Seventh

True Riches

Part 1

Tonight, I shall reflect on a matter of conscience. Not until my ordination as a priest and the early days of my ministry did my priorities around ownership bend irrevocably in favor of the poor. Prior to that, my family's monarchist leanings shaped my views on political and social matters.

On this page, after many years of ministerial experience, the Spirit urges me to share one particular incident that tipped me over the edge of what others expect from priestly example.

A major change in my moral vision occurred during an episcopal visitation to our remote parish in Chastelar. It began with my—some said—stubborn decision to travel to this remote, region of my diocese. My brother priests in and around Digne, the local authorities, and my dear Baptistine had sternly warned me of the dangers of such a trip.

Word had made its way down the mountain that bandit leader Cravatte and his gang of brigands—unwittingly redeemed and beloved children of our merciful God—had taken refuge in the mountains of Piedmont. The renegade troop had committed an audacious and sacrilegious crime in broad daylight.

Breaking into the cathedral of our neighboring diocese, the plunderers stripped the sacristy of its sacred objects and embroidered vestments, thereby adding to their mounting ill-gotten—now sacrilegious—treasury. This audacious crime warned the terrified populace that nothing and no one, not even the sacred temple of God, remained beyond the reach of their wanton plunder.

Undaunted by the general panic sown by this brazen act, I departed from Digne alone. Midafternoon, I arrived safely at a small town, the gateway to my final destination higher up the mountain.

The mayor met me with a furrowed brow. "I deeply regret, Monseigneur, I cannot risk the lives of my gendarmes to accompany you further. I respectfully advise Your Excellency not to travel beyond this hamlet."

"Thank you for your concern, Monsieur Mayor," I replied, "but on that mountain is a humble commune in need of my ministry. Beyond two years have passed since my last visit to these kind and honest folk. They deserve a personal visit from their bishop. I wish to assure them of God's love and my pastoral concern for their welfare."

"But Your Excellency," the good mayor objected before I raised my hand to beg his silence.

"What would they think of a bishop too frightened to go to them in their time of need? If you cannot provide an escort, I shall go on without one." I could see from the taut lines at the corners of the man's mouth that he disagreed. Observing the rare failure of his advice, that good man protested with a graver warning. "What if you meet up with that pack of wolves unprotected?"

He had only my safety in mind, but

my resolve hardened the more. "The wolves also need to hear from their bishop that God loves them," I said. "The Lord has called me here to serve them as well as the people of my diocese."

The mayor had a valid reason for concern. Meeting up with the Cravatte gang posed a genuine possibility. What defense would an aging bishop have, traveling alone through the brigands' staked-out territory? Had they not already demonstrated disdain for God and Church?

In truth, I looked forward to such an encounter, should it happen. Other than my life, I had nothing of great value for thieves to steal. I considered my physical safety of lessor concern than the peril to their own immortal souls.

Furthermore, who does not know how easy it is for the Church to replace a bishop? Bury one, another arrives to replace him. Life goes on.

I entered the village late in the day, unharmed, having encountered neither brigand nor saint along the way. Only God's birds and forest wildlife. During my visit, I offered the Holy Sacrifice of the Mass and led the people in prayer at the graves of loved ones recently deceased.

In my sermon, I exhorted old and young to devote themselves to generous service to one another. And, yes, with every breath I spoke of the goodness of our loving God. I urged them to keep the faith in this remote—now dangerous—outpost. I spent a long evening with the curé, sharing stories over a glass of pleasing regional wine. I empathized with this good priest's lonely struggle to remain faithful to his vocation in this island of families, loving each other, feeding their livestock, and scratching the earth for their daily bread. I saw myself in the role of Saint Paul's missionary companion, Joseph, to whom the great Apostle gave the quite appropriate name, Barnabas, meaning "the one who encourages" (Acts 4:24-37).

On the third day of my visit, we received disturbing news from a traveling merchant, who daily risked his life venturing from village to village in this forsaken corner of France. Cravatte and his outlaws, having already desecrated a cathedral, had ransacked several remote parish churches in that already hard-scrabble region of my diocese.

The frightened man made no effort to disguise his fear. "They recognize no authority, Your Excellency. They consider no place, however sacred, beyond their covetous grasp."

From his description of Cravatte's progress, I discerned that I had positioned myself directly in the bandit's path.

On the eve of my departure, after hearing the cure's confession, I begged him to hear mine. He did, with humility and consoling wisdom.

At the next morning's closing Mass, the congregation had just finished a rousing "Te Deum" when two horsemen galloped into the village square and stopped in front of the little wooden church.

A gasp of fear and dread dulled the sound of our chanted hymn. Congregants begged their Lord and Savior, Jesus Christ, for absolution of their sins, past and present. After depositing an unadorned wooden chest on the church steps, the riders remounted and, without a word, disappeared into the forest as rapidly as they had come.

The congregation buzzed with relief and anticipation.

"Who sent it?"

All knew, of course. Who else could it have been?

"What might the mystery chest contain?"

Some even cried out, "Snakes! Beware!"

Others, "A dead body!"

Most, including their pastor, sided with that final assessment. Some poor victim of the gang needed a Christian burial. No one, not even the curé, dared to open the box, fearing discovery of some horror. All eyes fell upon me. Accepting my unanimous election, I unlatched the top of the chest.

Within lay stolen ecclesiastical treasures. We soon learned from labels that the booty belonged to the Cathedral of Our Lady of Embrun! And this note:

"Cravatte to Monseigneur Bienvenu Myriel."

I remarked to the curé, "God has indeed provided for my safe return."

He shook his head. "Was it God, Monseigneur? Or Satan?" I replied with conviction, "Oh, it was God, my son. It was indeed our gracious God."

I returned to Digne with the chest resting on a cart drawn by my faithful donkey. Once home, I inspected the chest's contents. Inside, I found sacred vessels and other "treasures" of the violated cathedral.

I settled into my daily routine of

Mass, meditation, and visits to the hospital. I also dealt with tedious matters related to the administration of even a small diocese.

My mind, though distracted by activity, searched for the meaning of the central event of my journey to the bandit-infested mountains—and its implications or my future . . . and my soul. Through subsequent sleepless nights, I wrestled with the question of what to do with the purloined treasure I now held in trust for my neighboring bishop.

I had no part in stealing the jeweled vessels and ornate vestments, I reasoned. Nor had I any interest in keeping these goods or putting them to temporary use in our simply outfitted cathedral. Profiting from them in any personal way was out of the question. Common wisdom—supported by established civil law—demanded their return to the Bishop of Embrun.

The question nagging at my spirit was this: did any church truly need such treasures, even a cathedral? Did not our redeemer have nowhere to lay his head? What did he ever own beyond the garments that protected him from the elements?

He who changed water into wine kept

nothing for his own use or to sell. How great a sin could it be merely to alter the destination of the stolen goods by redirecting them to the poor, who needed them far more than another sacred space?

Final resolution of my moral dilemma came down to this: who needed this valuable cache the more, the cathedral from which it was stolen or those living temples of the Holy Spirit, the sick and dying in our sacred cathedral hospital, where our good sisters ministered to them day and night with the meager resources at their disposal?

On rereading the above paragraphs, I sense I may need to revise, not my ultimate decision, but my explanations to the curious and to potential critics. In the meantime, before retiring, I need to jot the few verses playing like a persistent melody, in and around my imagination. How they cry out for expression! I will get no rest this night if I do not tend to their demand for light and life.

Who Needs Them More?

stolen goods gift of bandits
offered in shadowy remorse
create their own dilemma
priority prevails but whose

whose the greater need
a destroyed temple
altars and broken glass
bereft of antique art

nearby sick and dying
shrines of failing flesh
sisters standing vigil
by alms alone sustained

who needs them
whose the greater cry
the answer clear
to one called bienvenu

The hospital was a low and narrow building of a single story, with a small garden. Three days after his arrival, the Bishop visited the hospital. The visit ended; he had the director requested to be so good as to come to his house.

"Monsieur the director of the hospital," said he to him, "how many sick people have you at the present moment?"

"Twenty-six, Monseigneur."

"That was the number which I counted," said the Bishop.

"The beds," pursued the director, "are very much crowded against each other."

"That is what I observed."

"The halls are nothing but rooms, and it is with difficulty that the air can be changed in them."

"So it seems to me."

"And then, when there is a ray of sun, the garden is very small for the convalescents."

"That was what I said to myself."

"In case of epidemics, we have had the typhus fever this year; we had the sweating sickness two years ago, and a hundred patients at times, we know not what to do."

"This thought occurred to me."

"What would you have, Monseigneur?" said the director. "One must resign one's self. This conversation took place in the gallery dining room on the ground floor.

The Bishop remained silent for a moment; then he turned abruptly to the director of the hospital.

"Monsieur," said he, "how many beds do you think this hall alone would hold?"

"Monseigneur's dining room?" exclaimed the stupefied director.

The Bishop cast a glance round the apartment and seemed to be taking measures and calculations with his eyes. "It would hold full twenty beds," said he, as though speaking to himself. Then, raising his voice: "Hold, Monsieur the director of the hospital, I will tell you something. There is evidently a mistake here. There are thirty-six of you, in five or six small rooms. There are three of us here, and we have room for sixty. There is some mistake, I tell you; you have my house, and I have yours. Give me back my house; you are at home here." On the following day the thirty-six patients were installed in the Bishop's palace, and the Bishop was settled in the hospital.

Fantine, Book the First, Chapter II, M. Myriel
Becomes Monseigneur Bienvenu

Chapter the Eighth

True Riches

Part 2

During the afternoon today, I again spent time in my small garden, as I often do during spring and summer months. I removed a few stealthy weeds encroaching upon our squash laden vines. I began by offering apologies to the weeds for terminating their precious lives. I needed to come to the aid of our luscious produce, my dear friends who help sustain my household. Plants must have access to needed water and sunlight. Is that not the universal mystery of life and death throughout our planet's animal and vegetable kingdoms? God desires that we humans integrate and harmonize each other's gifts and talents. We all know how difficult that has been from the very beginning in the Garden of Eden.

Resting a moment, I contemplated the mystery of my God dwelling in the heavens above and in the generous earth at my feet. With the west-leaning sun edging over my wide-brimmed straw hat—surely reddening the tip of my nose—an inspiration came to me: *I want you to write one more chapter on the difference between true and false riches.* In the silence of this latenight hour, a door opens to deeper understanding of negative attitudes and useless possessions. They clutter of daily life blocks our path to God. Negativity and possessiveness threaten to choke off gifts of divine grace, not unlike those weeds I cleared from my garden.

I have learned over time that my pre-waking moments provide especially fertile soil for the delivery of divine inspiration. This very moment, in fact, I hear another of those random, disconnected utterances. Through crusty, unfocused eyes, I reach for a scrap of paper, dip my quill pen in its fertile well and jot this seemingly random utterance for further consideration:

I cannot go through life a homeless beggar with an empty knapsack.

What could it mean? How to make sense of this random inspiration . . . "Going through life like a homeless beggar"? Still, I long ago vowed to embrace such out-of-the-shadows snippets for later revelation.

"Homeless beggar"?

"Empty knapsack"?

In God's good time and quite unexpectedly, a clue to its meaning just might appear in the form of a person in need, a soul desiring comfort and compassion. My position as bishop of a diocese does not allow me to roam the French countryside as an itinerant preacher, living off whatever alms the Lord provides in the course of a day. I have grave responsibilities. They bind me to this geographical place and time. I am responsible for the care of my flock, for management of church property and custody of precious donations.

In the nighttime silence of my bedroom, I experience a state of near paralysis. At the same time, my muse— all-wise Holy Spirit—compels me to record the fruit of my reflection on true riches. This moment in the writing process simultaneously terrifies and excites. In this state, everything becomes possible. I am a *tabula rasa*, an eager blank slate ever ready to receive inspiration.

As in prayer, I do well to avoid rehashing past deeds and misdeeds. Equally important, I must block any and all concern about obligations of the morrow. Nor dare I censor the thoughts and images that step from the shadows into this newly illumined space.

I close my eyes.

And breathe . . .

Into that emptiness appear images of my late, beloved wife. Not as I last saw her, being lowered into the life-rich Italian soil, but as the lovely, smiling *imago gaudii* I recall from our joyous wedding day. Yes, that's it exactly. . . she appeared visionlike, an image of unbridled, soon brided, joy if such a word exists. She still surprises me at in-between moments, like this, when spirits join in that neutral space where worlds converge but remain barely beyond reach, like Michelangelo's Adam in the Sistine Chapel.

How I long to touch her, hold her, express my eternal regret that I could not heal her, grant us a longer life together on peaceful French soil. We prayed for that every night before closing our eyes. In our youthful, blissful ignorance, we expected that very outcome when the end of our exile came to pass.

Now I see clearly. You, my gracious God willed that I should experience the ecstasy of my beloved's companionship, that I be schooled within the university of love in preparation for the second half of my life. Out of the desert of widowhood you called me, Lord Jesus, as the Holy Spirit called you to return from your forty-day desert retreat. You resurrected me to a most unexpected vocation as priest, promising a flower garden of spiritual children in place of those my wife's ill health and early passing denied us.

Looking back on my life, which I seem to do more frequently as I advance in age, I have come to understand and accept the truth that these seemingly disparate lives were not mean to be sequential—"this occurred . . . then that happened." My life story has revealed itself as single, divinely ordered continuum. My beloved taught me how to serve God as priest. I would never have been who I am today—what the Lord has made of me—had she not blessed my life.

How otherwise would I have learned the virtues of compassionate listening, patient endurance, and graceful suffering?

All is quiet now. Lovely, lyrical songs of God's night creatures spill through my open window. It is time to distill my thoughts into True Riches, Part 2. Pen in hand, I hover over the paper on my desk. At the top I write . . .

To the People of Digne and to Our Hospital Patients and Sisters . . .

When the Holy Father assigned me to the diocese of Digne, responsibility for managing two properties on the episcopal grounds became one of my greatest challenges. One spacious and airy, home to my predecessors. The other a smaller, overcrowded edifice, the medical institution under the care of our holy and wholly dedicated Sisters of Charity.

Compared to my inherited home with its many windows offering ample access to sunshine and fresh air, the other spoke of physical neglect and overcrowding. Not once did I see our nuns or their patients' envy, or worse, resent the episcopal residence—mine "by right of office." All that is good and decent compelled me to change an arrangement that was not only personally intolerable but sinfully unjust. I could not visit the sick, anoint those on the doorstep of death, and preside over their funerals, knowing my selfishness contributed to their final agony.

I needed so little space.

They deserved more.

I could not go on living, unless I changed that dynamic.

A gnawing discomfort settles in my chest, as I recall my sin of clinging to valuable relics of our family fortune. Out of place in the simple environment we created in our home was that set of silver dinnerware and the two matching candlesticks. These familial heirlooms traveled with me from parish to parish and now to my current residence. I kept those valuables in a closed, unlocked cupboard, reserved for those special but rare occasions when guests, invited or uninvited, dined with us. I often wrestled with their very presence among our family possessions.

In feeble defense, I cite my reluctant role as trustee of Myriel history and good fortune. I told myself I had a "duty"—the very title of this book—to keep them within the family. Through the years, they reminded me of the horrors my parents suffered during the revolution and its random brutality. As a secondary defense, I offered my responsibility to my beloved sister. I could not allow her to fall into poverty should she outlive me.

Last on my list, I had an inbred appreciation of the beauty of the objects themselves.

I shall now replace that list and begin anew.

Reasons for letting go of our family treasures:

On the one hand, those possessions challenged my commitment to adopt as my own the simple life of the people to whom I ministered.

Those inherited "treasures" nagged at my conscience. Who among my mostly peasant flocks possessed anything of such value? Barely a few? Perhaps none.

Who among them possessed anything of great value they might sell to extricate themselves from crushing debt?

Or to pay a doctor . . . or purchase medicine in times of grave illness?

Or, finance a hasty escape in the event of another eruption of France's cyclical political upheavals?

Having arrived at the bottom of that page, I shall conclude this examen with . . .

I always knew in the depth of my spirit that I dared not to hold our family treasures with a tight grip but as newborn sparrows hatching in the nest of my sun-warmed hands. Should the time ever come, I would free them to fly away.

How to predict that only days after making that pledge to my Redeemer, a disheveled, shunned, discarded soul would knock at my door seeking shelter and a morsel to eat? I had not foreseen that God's fated test of my unchallenged generosity would arrive so soon.

Perhaps the Lord did not trust my

resolve and thought it best to act
quickly, lest my generous mood
evaporate, like so many of the dreams
I strain to recall upon awakening . . .
but rarely do.

I must leave this chapter unfinished for now. It has grown later than I intended. I must appear refreshed and ready, Lord, to give you my best attention at Mass in just a few hours. But first, I feel obliged to jot in rough draft the verse that played at the back of my mind as I wrote. If I do not, my poor, tired brain may not hold the verses till morning and surely not as far distant as this time tomorrow night.

True Riches—2

silver and gold
in short supply
love and joy

abound as do

faith and hope

i know both

rich and poor

goods and things

have their place

but few abide

by diff'rent measure

I am possessed

of all bounty

by other metric

do I count

my riches true

Part the Second

Duties According to One's Life

Chapter the Ninth

Letter to the Romans

Sovereigns and Subjects: Obedience to Authority

"Let every person be subordinate to the higher authorities, for there is no authority except from God, and those that exist have been established by God. Therefore, whoever resists authority opposes what God has appointed, and those who oppose it will bring judgment upon themselves. For rulers are not a cause of fear to good conduct but to evil. Do you wish to have no fear of authority? Then do what is good and you will receive approval from it, for it is a servant of God for your good." — Romans 13:1-4

I faced a dilemma. Months ago. When outlining this book, I chose the writings of St. Paul, Apostle to the Gentiles. The Pauline letters store a treasure trove of wisdom regarding Christian obligations. I now wish to parse and write about some of them. My guide is that saintly preacher of early Christian *kerygma*—the essence of the mystery of salvation. In its most basic meaning, we can sum up our Christian faith with the following triad: Divinity took human flesh in Jesus; Jesus died on a criminal's cross; that same Jesus, rose from the dead and now reigns as our universal Christ.

So, I begin . . .

"Let every person be subordinate to the higher authorities, for there is no authority except from God, and those that exist have been established by God."— Romans 13:1 One's life map, beginning from the moment of conception, has both purposeful direction and symmetry. God's plan for each of us progresses according to a constant pattern. By that I mean, the elements of our life map shift as our context changes, seemingly at times by the day, teaching new lessons, sparking new insights. The Spirit of our Creator proves every day to be elusive, immune to capture, beyond definition, both in written word and spirit. However fervently we wish it were not so, the wet mortar of divinity refuses to set. From birth to death, we remain seekers, not possessors.

Know it or not, eternal Love quietly possesses us, whether we chart its presence and action in the moment or, go about oblivious of His presence, blithely living from day to day.

I am called again and again, it seems, to relive the life-changing events surrounding Jean Valjean's entrance into my life—brief though it was. During less than a twenty-four-hour period, the textbook distinction between sovereign and subject blurred for me.

Committed to a life of integrity, I flirted with lying to the very earthly authority I respected and to which Saint Paul himself counseled obedience. In that life-changing moment, our two disparate paths—Paul's and mine—intersected. Not until that moment did I understand how alike the two of us might be.

As a young man, I found myself, as never before, caught in the midst of a social and political struggle for power. Life in France during the late eighteenth and early-to-mid nineteenth centuries held its own peril for the those loyal to the Church of our birth and to what we held as, divinely sanctioned authority—whether monarch or other.

My country reeled from the revolution of 1789, when noble birthright, not personal guilt, set the standard for summary condemnation, imprisonment, even hideous and public execution. By this new standard, saints and sinners suffered equally.

The Valjean incident—consuming less than twenty-four hours of my life—began and culminated at my front door. That single experience altered my view of authority forever.

It began with a jolting knock on my residence door. Our little family—Baptistine, our housekeeper Madam Magloire, and I—had just blessed our meal and sat down to dinner. As man of the house, I rose to see who might call at this unusual hour.

Except in physical shape, the "being" filling our doorway barely qualified as human. What had sounded like the pounding of a sledgehammer, turned out to be the blunt edge of a wild-eyed, desperate wretch's massive, calloused fist.

"My name is Jean Valjean, I am a convict," the stranger announced with neither pride nor shame.

The name proved unfamiliar but not the man. In this uninvited visitor, I recognized the crucified Christ himself in the guise of a broken hulk, a wind-battered ship run aground on a foreign shore. Valjean had offered the simple truth of his name. His visage and manner revealed so much more. He needed a hot dinner, a clean bed. Both of which I had the means to supply. Above all, he sought restoration of his God-given, long-stolen humanity.

But hold! I dared not entertain my Lord in disguise with chipped dinnerware. My custom when receiving special guests was to set the table with our precious heirloom silver plates and matching candlesticks. The arrival of that long-suffering parolee qualified as just such an occasion. Though silent, Baptistine conveyed displeasure with a reflexive twitching at the corners of her mouth and dagger-like glances at the stranger . . .

and her brother.

I yielded my place at the head of the table to our guest of honor.

"You are good," he gurgled through greedy mouthfuls, "you don't despise me."

To which I responded in the language of deepheld conviction, "This is not my house. It is the house of Jesus the Christ"—therefore, your house too. "It asks not the name of any comer, only what his affliction might be."

For my part, I would gladly sleep in the shed, but the women under my protection deserved the dignity and safety of protected lodging.

Well past our retirement, I heard muffled sounds about the house. I remained as I lay. Fed and rested, Valjean—it could be no other—had risen sometime after midnight, I guessed. I heard him move stealthily through the dining room and, later, close the front door behind him. I had no need to confirm that he had vanished into the frosty night.

The following morning, I had just returned from early morning Mass when Madame Magloire wailed. "The silver is stolen!"

I countered her cries with a syllogism that quickly lost strength. "The silver belongs to the poor, not to us. Jean Valjean epitomizes abject poverty."

Ergo. . . .

As if on cue as part of a well-rehearsed theatrical production, a trio of gendarmes arrived, roughly dragging our houseguest along with a sack containing our purloined heirloom treasures. In that instant, Lord Jesus granted me the grace to tread the narrows of an intricate moral choice.

The gendarmes had discharged their duty. I held them not at fault. No civilized society can tolerate the anarchy of utter disregard for private property. On the other hand, the desperate thief faced a life sentence—possibly execution

—for taking something I would have gifted him with, had he but asked.

My moral choice: Which to favor? Sovereign or subject? Proportionality tipped the scale in favor of the accused.

I embraced my friend. "Ah, my dear Valjean! There you are, my friend. I am so happy to see you. I forgot to give you the matching candlesticks along with these plates. They will bring two hundred francs, at least. Now, take them, all of them."

To the gendarmes I added, "Sirs, it is all a mistake."

I read in the officers' eyes, those of

my sister, our housekeeper, and the stunned Valjean himself . . . it must be they who had misunderstood my intentions. But, how was that possible?

Their honest question remained unspoken—and unanswered.

I shall never forget our final moment together. As Jean Valjean prepared to depart in freedom, I leaned close to his ear and whispered what I can only describe as Spirit-planted words, reserved only for this one bewildered beggar.

"Never forget, Jean, you have promised me to use this silver to become an honest man. My brother, you belong no longer to evil, but to good. It is your soul I am buying for you, and I give it to God."

At my desk late that night, I contemplated what I had done. For the first time since assuming custody of the remnants of our family's earthly treasure. I thought about our plates and candlesticks. Not with the longing of regret, but with relief that I had taken a singular step toward identifying myself more closely with the condition of the majority of my flock. Having never rested comfortably in my possession, those objects offered greater joy in their absence than ever they did in my possession.

My only sorrow at the end of that most unusual day was that I might never again see my dear friend and beneficiary, the emancipated parolee Jean Valjean. Of course, I knew this not in the way a scientist reads the elements of earth.

In my years of pastoral experience, I have done what I could to feed at least a few of France's displaced vagabonds. In each case, I gave them a sous or two, bestowed my blessing, and sent them on their way to the next village and beyond. Most of them I have forgotten and might not recognize were I to encounter them today. Something about this one bereft child of God stirred in me what I can only call a "sacred boldness." Our Father-God seemed to have a message for just this man . . . and chose me as His heaven to earth postman.

Before putting away these freshly written pages, I read again my opening text from Romans. Why had I chosen it? With the question threatening to rob me of sleep, if not pursued, I open my well-worn Bible. My thumb guides these weary old eyes to Chapter Eight, verse thirty-five. "Who shall separate us from the love of Christ? Will it be trials, or anguish, persecution or, hunger lack of clothing, or dangers or sword?"

My heart returns to my twice-freed convict. Who dares to wonder that he rejected faith in a loving Christ? He who might never in his life have experienced a random act of kindness. At least, not during his many years of imprisonment—comprising every day of his adult life!

I take up my quill pen and write after the final words of my new chapter:

"Who or what shall separate us from the love of Christ?" Not stripping a man's name and substituting number 24601. Not two decades on the galleys. There is nothing those exercising brute power for ill can do to separate us from the love of Christ.

I pause halfway across the page . . . dip my pointed quill in the well . . . and press on.

Not the shunning of a parolee at every door in France.
Not even . . .

With a heavy stroke, I underline the last two words, concluding with . . .

disconnection from the decency and good- ness of our God-given humanity.

Weary now, I remove my black soutane and purple sash, loop the pectoral cross and chain over my head and, with reverence, press my lips to the image of my gentle Lord and Savior Jesus Christ, whose arms reach out to me in welcome. As is my custom, I kneel beside my bed, feeling the wooden floorboards press lines into my old knees. Instead of my usual night prayers, I recite Romans 8:38-39 . . .

"I am certain that neither death nor life, neither angels nor spiritual powers, neither the present nor the future, nor cosmic powers, were they from heaven or from the deep world below, nor any creature whatsoever will separate us from the love of God, which we have in Jesus Christ, our Lord."

* * *

Last night, not a poetic verse came to me. In prayer after Mass this morning, words rushed at me in a jumble. In the course of the day, the syllables took shape. Tonight, I dare not let the opportunity pass, lest this old, fragile brain not hold them.

Sovereigns and Subjects
on Romans 13:1-4

be they two or one
sovereign and subject
or mirror images of
one body whole

sovereign is beholden
to subject as subject
pays respect to
peace and order

each to sovereign
each in equality birthed
last shall be first
the first last

Chapter the Tenth

First Letter of St. Peter

"Though you have not seen (Jesus),
you love him; and without seeing him
now, you believe in him" —1 Peter 1:8.

On sunny afternoons, I enjoy sitting on the shaded bench in my garden. On this warming day, I opened my Bible to the First Letter of St. Peter. Among the twelve apostles, I admire Peter most. I see so much of myself in him—dedicated in love and service to his Master yet flawed to the point of betraying Jesus in his friend and mentor's hour greatest of need.

It is now close to midnight. I need my sleep and dread Baptistine's sisterly displeasure tomorrow morning if she suspects I have spent too much of the night in contemplation and writing. Nonetheless, I feel more impelled than ever to push forward, driven by a greater force than that possessed by my sister—should such exist.

In First Peter, the Apostle addresses Jewish Christians living in Asia Minor. Among the Twelve, those closest followers of the Lord, I identify most with the one Jesus called the Rock. I lay no claim to possession of Peter's heroic faith. Rather, I feel a strong connection with him, when I reflect on the great apostle's life and his initial letter to the Christians of his time. I reflect on the changes that came over the former Galilean fisherman in the three decades following the events of that terrible Friday—the one we now call Good. Why attach "goodness" to the horrendous events of that day? First, because we know how those tragic events ended—in glorious resurrection. Second, because we experience a hope-birthed faith that our own deaths will not mark the end of our personal story. Rather, we look forward to a joyous new beginning in another, unimaginable state of existence in Afterlife.

The Gospels reveal a sanguine Peter, one who sometimes vented his powerful emotions without measuring the consequences. He leapt to a physically violent response when his brother apostle, Judas, arrived at the Garden of Olives accompanied by the High Priest's armed thugs to arrest Jesus in the menacing manner of a long-sought fugitive. Rather than receiving gratitude from his lord and master, Peter absorbed this sharp rebuke, "Put your sword back in its place! For all who take hold of the sword will die by the sword" (Matthew 26:52).

Having sworn to stand with Jesus at the risk of life and freedom, within a few hours of his bold display, Peter thrice denied knowledge of his dearest friend, as chronicled by Matthew, his fellow apostle (26:69-74):

> As Peter sat outside in the courtyard, a young servant girl said to him, "You also were with Jesus of Galilee." He denied it before everyone, saying, "I do not know what you are talking about."
>
> Later, as Peter was going out through the gateway, another servant girl saw him and said to the bystanders, "This man was with

Jesus of Nazareth." Peter again denied it with an oath, saying, "I do not know the man."

After a little while, those who were standing there approached Peter and said to him, "Surely, you are one of the Galileans: your accent gives you away."

Peter began to justify himself with curses and oaths, protesting that he did not know Jesus. Just then, a cock crowed. By the time Peter wrote his initial pastoral letter, decades had passed. Shame and the humiliation of personal failure had sanded his rough edges.

The weight of his betrayal forever tempered his pride.

In the great apostle's later years, persecutions targeting adherents to the fledgling Christian movement within Judaism flared up in Rome and around the Empire. Erased were any utopian this-world expectations on Peter's part and that of all followers of the Risen Christ. Any hope of mass cross-cultural conversions and wholesale social change vanished. Persecution and death became ever-present threats to all who con-verted—those of Jewish origin equally with their Gentile brothers and sisters. Peter must have accepted the reality that his own life would soon provide fodder for the swirling madness of anti-Christian paranoia in the Empire.

I marvel that the apostle's concern in writing this first letter was not for his own safety but that of his brothers and sisters, now living in constant peril because of their beliefs.

I do not consider myself impulsive, although Baptistine—my second conscience—accuses me of that exact fault. She scolds me when I transgress her immovable boundaries of episcopal propriety. I confess that in my heart of hearts, I see myself as quite the opposite of Peter. I prefer to think before I speak. I gauge the path ahead when making decisions, searching out in advance any hidden pitfalls.

Clearly that trait disappeared when our local gendarmes dragged Jean Valjean back to my doorstep, along with the precious heirlooms they thought (correctly in the moment) he had stolen from our home. I do admit, what happened next caught even me off guard. On that too rare occasion, I discovered within myself the barest trace of St. Peter.

I am losing my train of thought. A sign that I would do well to put my quill pen aside and retire for the night. I must not waste good paper on random spiritual musings.

I write best and with greatest ease when the spirit of God bursts through my meandering distractions. Lately, the Lord has been quite active. I awaken each morning with eager anticipation of the day's surprises. I live in a state of high alert for unexpected encounters with the Risen Christ. It might occur during celebration of the Eucharist, but increasingly I discover God in the faith of a patient dying in our hospital. I see Christ in the out-stretched hand of a toothless beggar. I find him in the two faithful and devoted women who cook my meals and keep my house.

Tired as I am, I am compelled by a stronger voice to dip my pen once more and add at least a few additional insights gained from my afternoon meditation. Verse 8 of Chapter 1 in First Peter gives me pause, "Though you have not seen (Jesus), you love him; and without seeing him now, you believe in him" (1 Peter 1:8).

I imagine myself standing before a magnificent door. Once opened, it promises access to answers, at least in part, regarding one of life's greatest challenges and deepest mysteries—to believe or not to believe.

One of the great mysteries of the human spirit is our capacity to love an unseen lover. What is more, we can believe in something without ever seeing it with our physical vision. Of course, I have read and reflected on Peter's words in the past and often preached on them to the good folk of my diocese. Yet, each encounter with the same Scripture passage seems new, as if the words have appeared quite suddenly and fresh-inspired. Each time these particular texts in 1 Peter appear in the liturgy, their very newness moves me to validate that they are true in every way; the level of faith they demand is indeed humanly attainable.

At the risk of repeating what you have already read in this book, I must recall the day my father summoned me to his study and announced, without discussion, "Son, be glad. I have found you a suitable wife."

I responded with the only answer expected of a loyal, loving son. "I see. Thank you, Father."

I could think of no other response. The family name of my future wife was familiar, but I had never met this mysterious, "suitable" wife-to-be, whom I must accept and love until death would part us.

As I pondered my new reality over the days that followed, something strange occurred. I acknowledged, for the first time, it was time to take my future seriously. I promised myself and my unknown betrothed that I would take this step into responsible adulthood with all my being, a commitment which I and most of my cohorts had deliberately avoided.

During the days that followed, I contemplated my unforeseeable future. To my surprise, I discovered that I had room in my heart for a new presence, a life partner. The Marriage Sacrament meant Commitment and Fidelity. It also meant Responsibility and openness to Parenthood. I allowed myself the fantasy of cradling an infant in my arms. To my surprise, I experienced what I can only describe as the "first spark of love" in my heart. Yet, both my future wife and our yet to be conceived child existed only in my imagination. I marveled that I possessed a pre-disposition to hold each of them in growing affection and anticipation.

At that young age, I had not read First Peter. Much later, during a time of heightened distress, as my beloved wife's condition worsened, I came upon that mystical text, "Though you have not seen (Jesus), you love him; and without seeing him now, you believe in him."

In that instant, the apostle's insight rang true, and yes . . . I wept. If a young man can open his heart to a bride he has not seen and to a child they have yet to cocreate and experience a heavenly elation beyond all words, is it such a leap to love our unseen God? And find inexpressible joy in that discovery?

Unwittingly, I have written far too deep into this night, filling one page after another. More than once I have had to rewrite a portion of this chapter upon realizing that tumbling tears—could they truly be my own?—had smeared the ink. Again, this time of reflection calls me to close with a verse that rises from the pages just written.

The Magnificent Door
First Peter 1:8

not seeing my
Lord Jesus
how love him
not seeing
how believe

but hold . . . did
my heart not love
sight yet to see
the chosen bride
my longed-for bliss

sightless seeing
hopeful believing
soul's clear vision
fully assured
confident assent

being man
sight misleads
to Lord Christ
do i commit
doubt dispelled

Chapter the Eleventh

Letter to the Ephesians

Chapters 5:21 to 6:9

Let all kinds of submission to one another, become obedience to Christ.

So wives, to their husbands, as to the Lord. The husband is the head of his wife, as Christ is the head of the church, his body, of whom he is also the Savior. And as the church submits to Christ, so let a wife submit in everything to her husband.

As for you, husbands, love your wives,

as Christ loved the church and gave himself up for her. He washed her, and made her holy, by baptism in the word. As he wanted a radiant church, without stain or wrinkle or any blemish, but holy and blameless, he, himself, had to prepare, and present her to himself.

In the same way, husbands should love their wives, as they love their own bodies. He, who loves his wife, loves himself. And no one has ever hated his body; he feeds and takes care of it.

That is just what Christ does for the Church, because we are members of his body. Scripture says: Because of this, a man shall leave his father and mother, to be united with his wife, and the two shall become one flesh. This is a very great mystery, and I refer to Christ and the Church. As for you, let each one love his wife as himself, and let the wife respect her husband.

Children, obey your parents, for, this is right: Honor your father and your mother. And this is the first commandment that has a promise: that you may be happy and enjoy long life in the land.

And you, fathers, do not make rebels of your children, but educate them, by correction and instruction, which the Lord may inspire.

Servants, obey your masters of this world with fear and respect, with simplicity of heart, as if obeying Christ. Do not serve, only when you are watched, or in order to please others, but become servants of Christ, who do God's will, with all your heart. Work willingly, for the Lord, and not for humans, mindful that the good each one has done, whether servant or free, will be rewarded by the Lord.

And you, masters, deal with your servants in the same way, and do not threaten them, since you know that they, and you, have the same Lord who is in heaven, and he treats all fairly.

I close my Bible. It is time to reflect on St. Paul's words which I have just copied. I have listened to and preached numerous—too many?—sermons on the duties of wives and mothers and their responsibility for maintaining order and happiness in their homes. False preachers of my time (Lord, forgive me such a harsh judgment) justify their biased—to me, at least— pronouncements on the Apostle's admonition: "The husband is the head of his wife . . . . And as the Church submits to Christ, so let a wife submit in everything to her husband." My muse compels me to add my personal insights regarding this passage.

I consider it good fortune—divine grace, rather—that my experience as both husband and priest allows me to read and pray over the Apostle's passage on marital and parental love from a unique perspective.

Quite recently, I sat through a long and windy sermon on this text, delivered in my presence with lionlike roars. The iron-tongued preacher furrowed his brows and directed a severe admonition—with pointed finger—to our mostly female congregation. I could only close my eyes and release a distress-laden sigh. I thank my Lord for restraining me from springing to my feet and interjecting, "My dear brother, it would be so helpful to you and to all of us, if you knew what you were talking about." Paul did, in fact, address his remarks in Ephesians 5 mainly to husbands. He made very clear what it truly means to "love one's wife."

After Mass, I lingered on the cathedral steps greeting one family after another. I dealt sincere compliments on the appearance and behavior of their children. As I signed a blessing on the head of each little boy and girl, I told their mother in a code whose full meaning they intuit by nature, "Jesus understands." In weaker moments, I can only hope Jesus does, in fact, understand everything I have told people He does. In my better moments, I am positive of that.

I cite in my defense that in every case relief reflected in those mothers' eyes. I have witnessed immediate gratitude and

Recalling those good women and the miracle of their faith transports me to my early adulthood, especially to my personal experience of a love-filled marriage. By God's mysterious—providential—will, I did not have the joy of a flesh and blood child of my own.

As I shared in an earlier chapter, I

was barely out of my teens, when my father, whom I loved and respected, negotiated (yes, sadly, an exact description of the prevailing customs among our social class) a "fitting" marriage for his only son.

The successful revolution of July 1789 shocked the French monarchy and aristocracy. Being himself a dedicated monarchist, my father decided to send the newlyweds abroad to Italy. Bella Italia, he decided, offered the best hope of survival and a peaceful life. At least until the royalist forces quelled the "troubles," as he called them, and some semblance of normalcy returned. With winter approaching, the journey south across the Alps seemed less daunting to us than what we might face had we insisted on remaining in our turbulent native land.

Nightly, my bride's warm, inviting body tucked to mine for warmth on chilly nights, gave assurance that the ship of our predestined lives had set the two of us on course toward a safe— though foreign—harbor. We eagerly awaited the blessing of children. As you know, none arrived. Would it have been different had we remained in Paris?

If I had the responsibility of caring for children, I would not be who I am today. I heard my Lord urging me then to turn my "what ifs" over to him. I did and continue daily to obey God's will for my life.

We settled finally in the Holy City, Rome—teeming capital of a strange new land populated by beautiful, warmhearted people. Our social status meant little to our new "famiglia," who welcomed us into their hearts and homes. Being Catholics, we attended Mass on Sundays but gave little thought to the deeper invitation to interior spirituality. Nor did we place much emphasis on the penitential practices of our baptismal faith.

Then, something changed. In the numbing emptiness of my status, I became conscious for the first time of the great distance separating me from my family and the camaraderie of supportive friends. Having emigrated from nearly faithless France to Rome, the atmosphere of sacred art and architecture spoke to my long-dormant spirit.

I found myself caught up in its history, both pagan and Christian. I sought solace and shade from the midday sun by visiting the nearby Basilica di Santa Francesca Romana. That historic tenth-century edifice sat atop the site once dominated by the Temple of Venus. Shortly after that first visit, I began attending Sunday Mass with that community, mostly to provide a marker separating one lonely week from another. I don't recall the exact date it began, but not long after, I sought solace through attendance at daily Mass. The spirituality in and around that sacred space became the oxygen of my rebirth.

Emerging day by day from the blind hole of grief, as from a self-dug grave, I experienced, of all things, a gradual and quietly surprising call to study for the priesthood. In those priests I met and got to know, I found a selfless dedication to service and commitment to improving the lot of their parishioners.

Overcoming my initial shock at such a development, I responded with all my soul but, I am embarrassed to admit, not before bargaining with God on one point. I share the following prayer— or "spiritual barter," if you prefer—with no pride but only for the sake of truth. "I will give you my life, Lord Jesus, but . . . allow me cling to my treasured memories of married life and carry with me the image of my beloved: a radiant smile lighting her face and finding its 'other' in mine."

Hearing no objection from on high, I sought admittance to Holy Orders. As a seminary student, I plunged into the sacred disciplines, reading Augustine, Aquinas, Bonaventure, and other great theological minds of the past.

As a newly minted priest, I found my greatest joy in hands-on ministry among Rome's poor and suffering. The only advanced degree I sought was the embossed golden seal of the *Collegium Vitae*. In that School of Life, I measured my value not by titles and capital letters after my name but by other less glamorous standards . . . compassion, understanding, humility. Within those sacred halls, I have loved and been loved body and soul for half a century. I fear that this preamble to Ephesians 5:21 to 6:9 will require some trimming as a I move through future drafts of this work. But I shall let it stand for now.

Husbands

I am inclined to pass over what Ephesians says about a wife's responsibilities. The filter of my soul allows only these words to pass from

Spirit to paper:

> "Husbands, love your wives
> as Christ loved the Church
> and gave himself up for her.
> . . . Husbands should love
> their wives as they love their
> own bodies. He who loves
> his wife loves himself."

The Apostle to the Gentiles sees greater urgency and need to address Christian husbands, rather than wives. Was St. Paul speaking from personal experience? Quite likely, in light of his education from childhood to young adulthood as a strict Pharisaic Jew. Perhaps he had been widowed, like me. Or, I wonder, had his wife looked with disfavor upon her post-Damascus stranger? It does not strain the imagination to think that many orthodox Jews might have refused to associate themselves with her apostate husband. If so, this made life quite difficult for the good Jewish woman. She might have separated from him to maintain her status within her local synagogue community.

No one seems to know for certain. I, for one, like to think that Paul and I share the common experience of marital life. I say this because he put forward his inspired, enlightened expectations and advice to converts emerging from prevailing pagan marital practices that reduced women to an inferior status.

A pagan wife had minimal rights and little protection should her husband die, leaving her bereft of male protection and without a male heir to assume responsibility for her safety and welfare. These same biases applied to bereft Jewish women. In Jesus' final will and testament, uttered from the cross, did he not appoint John to care for his widowed, soon to be childless mother, lest she be left alone and defenseless?

"Near the cross of Jesus stood his mother, his mother's sister Mary, who was the wife of Cleophas, and Mary of Magdala. When Jesus saw the mother and the disciple whom he loved, he said to the mother, 'Woman, this is your son.' Then he said to the disciple, 'This is your mother.' And from that moment, the disciple took her to his own home.—John 19:25-27

Tonight, these verses burrow into my heart, causing tears to well. Lord, from whence my involuntary weeping?

Fathers

I confess to feeling less confident about parsing a verse that follows a few lines deeper into Ephesians:

"And you, fathers, do not make rebels of your children, but educate them, by correction and instruction, which the Lord may inspire."

I had no son to guide into adulthood in France's fractured and increasingly unsettled society. Nor had I a cherished daughter to protect and upon whom to lavish my paternal affection.

I suffer a moment of distraction from my text. I cannot help but wonder about Jean Valjean. Did he marry? Is he now a father? I hope so. Hope is all I have, since I have not seen him since the day he relieved me of our burdensome family treasures. Such is the life of a pastor of souls. Ours is not to cling but to heal and send people off with our blessing to live their lives for good or ill. Wiping my eyes on my sleeve, I carry on. . .

I have never suffered the scorn of a rebellious adolescent child on the cusp of adulthood. Still, my years in ministry have taught me that neither the Bible nor world literature, ancient or modern, has solved the mystery of delicate, often abrasive parent-child relationships. The

Great Apostle knew this. How could his own father not have been ashamed of his conversion to Israel's sworn enemy, those Jesus Jews, as some called them, now infiltrating their synagogues as if still possessing the right to worship with lifelong, faithful Jews?

My own father—may God rest his soul—never understood how I could forego a second marriage and give him the grandson he so desired. Do I give myself too much credit believing I would have been a less rigid father than he, no matter the vocations my children spent their lives pursuing?

Children

I feel called by the spirit of St. Paul to put in writing something I have never shared with anyone. Yet, I hesitate. Who on this planet we call home would understand what I wish to share? Who would not misunderstand? Yet, the Apostle's voice cries out within me to allow myself a private admission, one I promised myself would never find its way to daylight. Yet here I am, about to reveal it to you, my unknown reader. All I ask is that you receive it with a kind and gentle spirit.

The lingering pain of childlessness is such that, wherever my ministry takes me, I search for glimmers of my likeness or that of my wife in the face of every child I encounter. Foolishness? Guilty! As priest, now prelate of the Church, albeit of little consequence in the hierarchical scheme of our Universal Church, I treat those entrusted to my care the way I would hope to have treated those who shared my flesh and blood.

In prayer, I aspire to affinity with the loving father of the "prodigal" son in Luke 15. This most touching of Jesus' volume of sacred parables revealed the kind of God who lays paternal claim to the human race. Day by day, I keep watch for the Christ disguised in the tattered garb of a prodigal. They come to me seeking—praying for—a compassionate path to reconciliation. Like that exemplary father in the gospel, I cleanse them with tender welcome—and a hot meal.

I am reminded—once again—of Jean Valjean. I called him "my son," as I have countless others over the years. Yet, this one encounter haunts me as no other.

"My son."

That is how I shall address him when we meet in that Paradise he no longer believed in on the day he crossed our threshold and entered not just my home and hearth, but indeed the innermost recesses of my heart.

Glancing toward the small dresser near my bed, I see the ewer and basin from whose chilled contents I will wash in the fast-approaching morning. These household items trigger an image. Did not St. Paul, in imitation of Christ, become the quintessential servant to the growing community of new believers?

"I am being poured out as a libation over the sacrifice and the offering of your faith, yet I rejoice and continue to share your joy; and you likewise should rejoice and share my joy" (Philippians 2:17-18).

Employing that simile, the apostle declared his ministerial motivation as an example and measure for all. He taught bywords and by the life he lived, in Christ. From the shallow drawer beneath the surface of my writing table, I remove a miniature image of my wife. Though no artist of any real talent, I painted it on one of her better days, before that cruel, uncaring illness took permanent hold. My only fiction was to splash a rosy blush upon her cheeks. She glances toward my episcopal robes neatly arranged in the open armoire. I imagine her smiling. "For you to become who you are," she whispers, "I needed to withdraw from this life. Had I not, we would still be together. What a great loss that would be to the people you serve."

I brush yet another tear that has rained on the forest of my bearded cheek and again take up my quill pen.

Servants

From Christianity's beginning, continuing into my own lifetime two millennia later, abuse of power and accumulation of personal wealth by churchmen have clouded the core message of Jesus. On the day of my ordination,

I swore this personal vow: If I am to find happiness again in this life, dear Lord, let it be in humble servanthood. Since my appointment as Bishop of Digne, a doubt has nagged at the edges of my spirit. To what extent have title and the trappings of ecclesial office tarnished my original good intent?

I must yield to my body's plea for sleep. I have more to say on this subject of blessed servitude, but it must await another time. As a personal period at the end of this chapter, I close with:

Ephesians 6:1-9

husband
love your wife
with her be one
to behold in awe
in being and blessing

children
gift of new life
full of dreams
potential awaiting
turn to shine

servants
among God's chosen
achieving in flesh
the goal of all
service to servants

newborn believer

dismissing now

darkness of disbelief

knowing truth

truth i share

At last, I pull warming bed covers to my chin. May the Lord grant me at least a few hours' peaceful rest, before Baptistine raps on my door, and it is time to rise for morning Mass.

Good night, dear Lord. Let your angels cover this dwelling with a blanket of restful peace. If I have offended you in any way today, I beg forgiveness and mercy. Amen

Chapter the Twelfth

Letter to the Hebrews

Part 1

Seated on our garden bench this afternoon, I leafed through the sacred text at rest in my lap. First, I came upon this amazing passage from Psalm 8, verses 3 to 6:

> When I observe the heavens, the work
> of your hands,
> the moon, and the stars you set
> in their place—
> what is man, that you

be mindful of him;
the son of man, that you should
care for him?
Yet, you made him a little less
than a god;
you crowned him
with glory and honor
and gave him the works
of your hands;
you have put all things
under his feet—
sheep and oxen without number,
and even the beasts of the field,
the birds of the air, the fish
of the sea,
and all that swim the paths
of the ocean.

O Yahweh, our Yahweh,
how great is your name
all over the earth!

A frisky midafternoon breeze leaped the wall to refresh our grounds and nearby convent. It shoos away the intense heat prevailing when I first came out to pray. I welcome the dancing air flapping my hat's wide brim. As if possessing fingers, it flips to the inspiring second chapter of the Letter to the Hebrews. Scholars have long attributed this letter to St. Paul. Some few "modern" exegetes, I understand, are questioning the apostle's authorship. Until they settle the matter convincingly within the halls of biblical academia, I shall continue to envision Paul as the inspired author.

The stellar prose reveals a dazzling catechesis wrapped in a loving embrace of poetic verse. Contented, I lower my eyes and begin at Chapter Two, verse one.

We must pay the closest attention to the preaching
we heard, lest we drift away.

Could not the good Lord have commanded the breeze to select a less challenging text? With body and spirit comfortable to the point of sluggishness, I feel more inclined to drift away than pay attention. Soon, my inner voice steps forward to address my weakness without subtlety: "By what right do you command the Author of Life to function within your limited parameters?"

My thoughts fly to the prophet Elijah. Exasperated by failure, the prophet found a cave in which to hide from Yahweh. The comparison amuses me. With my left thumb bookmarking my place in Hebrews, I flip to First Kings 19:11-14. There I find a frightened and weary Elijah hiding from Yahweh. I understand the prophet's mood. At times in my ministry, Lord Jesus, I too share his desire to hide from you.

> *There was first a windstorm, which rent the mountains and broke the rocks into pieces before Yahweh, but Yahweh was not in the wind. After the storm, an earthquake, but Yahweh was not in the earthquake; after the earthquake, a fire, but Yahweh was not in the fire; after the fire, the murmur of a gentle breeze.*
>
> *When Elijah perceived it, he covered his face with his cloak, went out, and stood at the*

entrance of the cave. Then he heard a voice addressing him again, "What are you doing here, Elijah?"

He answered, "I am burning with jealous love for Yahweh, the God of Hosts, because the Israelites have forsaken your Covenant, thrown down your altars and slain your prophets with the sword. No one is left but myself, yet they still seek my life to take it away."

Yahweh God, you appeared to Elijah not in the form of a howling wind. Nor did the soul-weary prophet recognize your majestic presence during a violent shaking of the earth beneath his feet. The upheaval threatened to entomb him forever. Not even in the firestorm that followed did Elijah find his God. Instead, the prophet recognized you "in the murmur of a gentle breeze."

A familiar voice addressed him, "What are you doing here, Elijah?"

The prophet could only raise his arms heavenward in surrender and show himself at the entrance of the cave.

Today, the Lord's plaintive question touches me deeply. I sit, not in a dark cave, but in this lovely, pine-shaded portion of our garden. The divine query nags me to ask, "What am I *doing* here?" or better, "What am I doing *here* . . . in this place . . . this time in history?"

My question flows from ceaseless puzzlement about my early life as a young student, my subsequent marriage, especially my wonder at God's unexpected and delayed call to priesthood. On my wedding day, I thought God Almighty had chiseled my life's path in that same Carrara marble I came to admire during our Italian exile.

In the aftermath of my beloved's death, had not God's call to ministry reached me in the timeless stillness of a gentle Roman breeze? In that refreshing embrace, I sensed, as the Hebrews called it, *ruah*—the "breath" of the Holy Spirit.

*   *   *

As my prayer time ended this afternoon, I closed my eyes, letting Yahweh's question to Elijah—and me—purge my shortsightedness. Tonight, in my only private space, I pray that my increasingly selective memory will retain this afternoon's inspirations.

The flicker of a single candle provides—barely—sufficient light by which to read and write. These nightly tasks I find more challenging as I age. As I ink my quill pen, I experience again the familiar fleeting terror I experienced when facing the very first blank page.

Chapter 2, Verse 6

The author of Hebrews writes for an audience of Jewish converts to solidify faith in their newfound Messiah, Jesus the Christ. Here, he quotes from their familiar Old Testament poetic prayer-song, Psalm 8, verses 4-10.

When I observe the heavens,
the work of your hands,
the moon, and the stars
you set in their place—
what is man, that you
be mindful of him;
the son of man,

that you should care for him?
Yet you made him
a little less than a god;
you crowned him with glory and honor
and gave him the works of your hands;
you have put all things
under his feet—
sheep and oxen without number,
and even the beasts of the field,
the birds of the air,
the fish of the sea,
and all that swim the paths
of the ocean.
O Yahweh, our Yahweh,
how great is your name
all over the earth!

"What is man?"

Such biblical conundrums never fail to nag at me for attention. I have long grappled with this question of personal identity and now set my whole inner being to the task of breaking open its inner meaning. The outrageous disproportion of the equation stuns me. Creator of the universe. The Creator-Owner of the vast universe, with all its interstellar space, showing individual concern and care for little Earth's innumerable creatures, both living and inanimate.

Humanly speaking, it is arrogance—fantasy—to expect that same God to care for me, as a unique being living in a remote corner of France. Can it truly be one such as I whom the Creator cares about? Even when I engage both mind and heart in feeble, imperfect prayer?

Each time I ask, I receive the softest whisper (ruah). The gentle breath of God provides the only possible answer to my query:

"You wish to know why I care, Charles? My only reason is this: I just do. I am who I am. I shall not have another mind about loving you—ever."

The twenty-sixth verse of chapter 6 in

St. Matthew's Sermon on the Mount rushes to consciousness:

"Look at the birds of the air: they neither sow nor reap nor gather into barns, and yet your heavenly Father feeds them. Are you not of more value than they?"

This verse offers a contemplative segue to Yahweh's response to that giant among all prophets, Isaiah. In 49:15-17, we marvel at Yahweh's tender words of compassion and encouragement to the exiled Hebrews:

Can a woman forget
the baby at her breast,
have no compassion
on the child of her womb?
Yet though she forget,
I will never forget you.
See, I have written your name
upon the palm of my hands;
your walls are ever before me.
Your sons hurry back,
and those who laid you waste
hasten to depart from you.

"I have written your name upon the palm of my hands." Perhaps the most beautiful and stunning metaphor in all of Scripture!

We stand today at the marker of nearly four millennia of intimate divine involvement, "indwelling" we call it, with the human spirit. Still, those words of divine-human, Judeo-Christian history define the cornerstone of our faith. It is that simple . . . and that unfathomably complex. Lord, you cannot help loving me nor I you. I have no doubt who fares the better in this exchange.

When I give free rein to the indwelling Holy Spirit, there seems no end to the sparks that fly in all directions as from a newly stoked campfire. My personal inspirations, originating from someone else, in this case a divinely inspired author, take on a life of their own. But those moments are not the norm. Most often, I struggle my way through a chapter, trying—perhaps too hard—to find just the right word or expression. This is one such night. I cry out (soundlessly), "At this pace, how will I ever finish this book?"

The Author of All's response sent a jolt through my body. "Would it be such a terrible thing, Charles, to leave your book unfinished?"

Humbled, I admitted to myself as much as to the Lord, "In the grand scheme of the universe, it would not."

In a moment of light, I perceive the value of the writing process itself. What I am doing through all these late-night sessions has value within itself. I will continue to write, even if my final decision is to hold these pages in sole my possession, for my eyes only.

I return my pen to its well. With eyes closed for a few moments, I surrender to sorely needed, if fleeting, rest.

Chapter 2, Verses 16-18

The divinely inspired author continues:

Jesus came, to take by the hand, not the angels but the human race. So, he had to be like his brothers and sisters, in every respect, in order to be the high priest, faithful to God and merciful to them, a priest, able to ask pardon and atone for their sins. Having been tested through suffering, he is able to help those who are tested.

I will let someone better schooled than I parse the deeper theology of Hebrews. Being at heart and by ecclesiastical assignment a pastor of souls, I feel called instead to probe the writer's heart. Let me ponder the image of Lord Jesus taking the human race "by the hand." I marvel at the comfort I receive from this intimate divine-human linkage.

I do everything possible to share this with the good people of the Diocese of Digne. I can only hope and pray that my words and actions invite their embrace of the image . . . and gently grasp our Savior's nail-punctured hands, extended to them in their hour of need.

Jesus did not hesitate to physically touch the people he encountered, some to greet, others to heal. He even accepted without struggle the fatal Judas kiss in the Garden of Gethsemane.

Prior to my marriage, under the scrutiny of unsmiling chaperones, my betrothed and I rarely touched each other. On our wedding day, at the altar of eternal union, I reached for my new bride's hand and felt her respond with subtle but matching enthusiasm. Dare I say it, with passion? In her eager touch, something new took possession of my heart—my whole being. She offered me a foretaste of her warm, inviting embrace and that of my, as yet unfamiliar, Crucified Lover. Before she had completed her sacramental vow with, "I take you, Charles, as my husband, until death."

I received a fleeting awareness of a far greater truth. In our flesh, Jesus the Christ had grasped our hands . . . the likes of us! With a firm grip, he vowed his own promise of lifelong fidelity.

Until that life-changing moment, my only thought had been of my good fortune and the anticipated pleasure of making love to my wife for the first time . . . and ever after, till death would us part. Death. The concept meant nothing to me then. That glorious day, I begged "death" to delay its visit to our home for many, many years. It's coming was inevitable but surely decades in the future, at a time when our marriage had ripened and borne fruit—children, grandchildren, perhaps even great-grandchildren.

Death decided against committing to such a promise, with other as yet unforeseen fates for both of us. It is better, is it not, that we cannot see our futures in advance.

A second memory pulls me forward to a sadder, more troubled time. As my wife neared death, I sat on the edge of our bed of ecstasy and sorrow. Taking her limp fingers in my palms, I pressed them to my lips, recalling in that moment how we as young lovers had joined our bodies with passionate urgency to conceive a child. As one sterile year followed upon another, our lovemaking lost, not ardor but worse . . . hope.

These events and my awareness of them have lain dormant for many decades. Only ripening maturity has surfaced them to consciousness, providing hard-won understanding and acceptance. The same Christ who first stretched out his hands to us on our wedding day . . . grasped our hands with greater urgency as she lay dying.

On the first occasion, the Lord bound Himself with us in mutual commitment. On that latter day, he reminded us our separation would be temporary. The time of our loss would flash at lightning speed and culminate with our joyful reunion in Paradise. Confidence that we will join together again sustains me to this day.

I kneel daily in private before the Blessed Sacrament, praying my own silent Te Deum.

This morning, kneeling before the high altar in the cathedral, I prayed again those solemn words: "We praise thee, O God; we acknowledge thee to be the Lord." I had one hour to ponder and pray before celebrating weekday Mass for the handful of faithful, mostly women, who attend each day. The unpadded prie dieu chafed my shins, even through the coarse wool of my soutane. Refusing to be silent, my knees squeaked off-key complaints at a lifetime of supporting my ample weight.

I opened my Bible to Hebrews, Chapter 3, and read in silence a verse drawn from Psalm 95. When our elderly sacristan made his way to the main altar with a lighted taper, I noticed a limp. He bore without complaint this daily Reminder of an injury received long ago in one of Napoleon's greed-driven wars. His pre-Mass task signaled the end of my meditation, but with the reassuring thought that tonight I would have much to write about.

Chapter 3, Verse 7

"Listen to what the Holy Spirit
says: 'If only you would hear
God's voice today!'" — Psalm 95

Explore with me the mystery of our
God's authentic "voice." The author
drew inspiration from the Old Testament
Psalm. Converted Jews of the early
Jesus movement had every intention and
right to remain loyal to the faith of
Abraham, Isaac, Jacob, and Moses,
as did Saint Paul, the Apostle to the
Gentiles, during his entire post-
conversion lifetime.

Indeed, through all my personal post-"conversion" life, I have faced the challenge of distinguishing the human word from the divine. Except for those rare occasions of direct communication, God's voice is mediated to me primarily through Nature, human interaction, and Scripture. That is my challenge, as it is every human's quest. The difficulty lies in the all-too-finite mediation of the Eternal Infinite through fickle earthlings, assumed to be the "crown of creation."

Once attuned, I find it easier to discern God's voice speaking through those parts of Nature we humans, with our seemingly incessant wars, have yet to defile beyond recognition. Each rising sun invites me to choose life with the words of Psalm 118, "This is the day the Lord has made; so, let us rejoice and be glad."

When baptizing an infant, I study the baby's eyes. In them, eternity comes into view. I catch a glimpse of the Creator from whose hands the newborn has arrived and been committed to the custody of parents dedicated to providing for this miracle of new life.

Clarity of vision fades when mediated by imperfect adults like me. In my boyhood, my father taught me his personal dogma: "It is the king's role and duty to reflect God in matters of state; the pope and his cardinals in matters of faith . . . only." Leaving adolescence behind and treading among the hazards of my adult years, I surrendered such romantic and flawed idealism.

Too much blood has been shed in the name of kings and church leaders alike in the defiled name of our God. So many, during my unfinished lifetime, have surrendered their precious lives on battlefields, in prisons, and street uprisings. One might rightly wonder how Christianity has survived at least mostly intact, into the late eighteenth to the mid-nineteenth centuries—my life span. I thank the Holy Spirit unceasingly for refusing to let humans silence forever the original "kerygma," the core message of God's enduring love, a love that led His Son to the cross for our salvation.

As Jesus predicted in the Sermon on the Mount (Matthew, Chapters 5-7), the most trustworthy mediators of the voice and message of God are those among us who live marginalized lives, namely, the outcasts, those biblical "anawim," or, as we call them in France, "les miserables." In their knock at my door, I hear a divine summons to respond with the compassion and love of our now Risen and Glorified Christ.

To see my God, I have only to visit the hospital next door and gaze into the surrendering eyes of a dying patient. In the pleas of beaten-down, homeless beggars and the unheard weeping of brutally imprisoned convicts, I hear the voice of God crying for mercy and some shred of justice. One cannot help thinking of Matthew's vision of the Last Judgment in Chapter 25, verses 38-40. The evangelist complements the Beatitudes, laying the saving burden of social justice directly upon our shoulders:

The King will say to those on his right: "Come, blessed of my Father! Take possession of the kingdom prepared for you from the beginning of the world. For I was hungry, and you fed me, I was thirsty, and you gave me drink.

I was a stranger, and you welcomed me into your house. I was naked, and you clothed me. I was sick, and you visited me. I was in prison, and you came to see me." Then the good people will ask him: "Lord, when did we see you hungry and give you food; thirsty and give you drink, or a stranger and welcome you, or naked and clothe you? When did we see you sick or in prison and go to see you?"

The King will answer, "Truly, I say to you: whenever you did this to these little ones who are my brothers and sisters, you did it to me."

As he is wont to do, Jean Valjean rushes to mind as the prototype of all my brothers and sisters whom society has cast to the bottom of the human pit. That wild-looking stranger entered and passed through my life, never to be heard from again. I have chronicled in previous chapters the story of this one convict's plight which so moved me that I responded to the Holy Spirit's spur-of-the-moment prompt to unload the nagging burden of our family treasure. I still pray for him each day.

When we meet in heaven, I expect we will have a very, very long talk. I long to hear the rest of his life story, beginning from the day he disappeared from my life. It now seems certain this face-to-face encounter shall not take place in this life.

I breathe an *Amen*, but before preparing for sleep, I must obey my private muse and write . . .

A Single Candle

A single candle
offers light

illumining my
nightly display
of meager wisdom

Hebrews 2:6
"what is man, that you be mindful
of him; the son of man, that
you should care for him"

why do i bother
with you Jesus
why do i care
a simple answer
only in you
i find my self

Hebrews 2:16-18
"Jesus came to take by the hand,
not the angels but the human race"

reaching not for
angel's grasp
you search
humble fingers
palms upturned

Hebrews 3:7
"Listen to what the Holy Spirit says:
'If only you would hear God's voice today!'"

not despair but sadness
in Spirit's 'if only'
yearning to unplug
faulty hearing of a
whispered 'there's more'

With these final strokes, I have no energy left to write, not even one more word. Putting tonight's pages into my desk drawer, I offer thanks to my sacred muse, none other than you, my Lord Jesus Christ. I pray that I write only what you want—no more, not a word less.

Chapter the Thirteenth
Letter to the Hebrews

Part 2

Faith is the assurance of what we hope for, being certain of what we cannot see. Because of their faith, our ancestors were approved. By faith, we understand that the stages of creation were disposed by God's word, and what is visible came from what cannot be seen.

— Chapter 11, verses 1-3

I return to these essential words of Saint Paul (likely not for the last time).

As a boy, I possessed a lively imagination. Immersed in Homer's Iliad and Odyssey, I envisioned myself as Achilles, the mighty and fearless warrior. In early adolescence, my fascination shifted to the lives of heroic saints. Especially, did those early Christian martyrs capture my idealistic imagination. Deacon Stephen—the first Christian known to have surrendered his life in defense of his commitment to the Risen Christ. And Sebastian, a third-century Gallic soldier, an officer in the legions of Rome—a secret Christian—

later martyred for his faith in a hail of body-piercing arrows, as if he were a common pin cushion. These were not mythic warriors but real men, who gave all in fidelity to Christ.

My man-of-the-world father, though Catholic by baptism, deemed harboring, as he called them, "spiritual dreams" and "fantasies of faith" as character flaws in a young nobleman. He trusted in science and the king, with preference for the latter. Deferring to father's wishes and example, I confined spiritual idealism to the remote recesses of my soul.

As I grew to adulthood and began advanced studies, I immersed myself in university follies (yes, carousing), bold but empty political discourse, and, finally, an arranged marriage. Though too blind to discern it at the time, I had traveled far along the path of molding myself in my own father's dreaded image and likeness.

The relative idleness of life in exile spurred within me a renaissance of imagination. I spent whole days exploring the churches and museums of Rome and the Vatican. Sculptures retrieved from ancient Greece, some limb-deprived, stole my breath. As did the masterworks of Michelangelo di Lodovico Buonarroti Simoni. I love the lilting poetry of that name. It flows so musically off the tongue. His Moses and Pieta, along with the works of other Renaissance masters captured my soul. Reconnection with the sacred through classical art sent me exploring—of all things—the Sacred Scriptures that inspired so many of these otherworldly masterpieces. After a long hiatus, I again sought moral courage and inspiration in the lives of saints.

Even these many years later, I recall a particular day on which I sought respite from the oppressive Roman heat within the storied Sistine Chapel. Clusters of silent tourists came and went. I found an open space apart from the foot traffic and stretched out on the floor, eyes to the frescos adorning the chapel's vaulted ceiling.

This violation of protocol drew scolding "tsks" from a passing sacristan, who nonetheless did not command me to assume a more respectful posture. Perhaps, I thought, this man had done the same as a youth and knew it as the only way to meditate upon Michelangelo's beyond magnificent frescoes. Such indulgence earned the understanding gentleman a generous stipend on my way out. Gazing at this Bible in the sky, my spirit soared beyond the boundaries of my physical body. My breathing slowed. I did not—could not—pull back, being powerless to discipline my contemplation. The very act of writing these words revives that thrilling moment in which my spirit left my body and soared to the vaulted ceiling.

Adam—"Man"—seemed unsure about accepting his creator's gift of life. His index finger curled slightly downward, whereas the finger of Creator-God showed no hesitation to share Spirit . . . Intelligence . . . Life . . . with this new creature on whom He bestowed the capacity to think . . . to love . . . to choose . . . and therefore, sadly, to sin.

In that trance-like state, I envisioned

myself in that scene and prayed:
"If only I could take Adam's place in the Garden. I would extend my finger toward You, my Creator-God."

Perhaps my outstretched fingers might succeed where the first man's failed, closing that narrow gap between God and man.

In that instant, I received a lightning bolt of grace. "Creator and sustainer of all life," I prayed, "let me become once more the true believer of my early youth." Our two index fingers strained to meet in space—one divine, the other all too similar to Adam's. Sadly, my reach fell even shorter than his.

Waking from my reverie, the desire

to erect a scaffold seized me. If only I could climb all the way to the ceiling, as the inspired artist had. I envied the one whose creative brush and sensitive flesh had touched God's outstretched finger, in which all power on heaven and earth resided.

Time passed.

How much? My only measure was the movement of shifting shadows cast across the eastern wall from high windows opposite.

I rose to a sitting position, flexed my knees, and stood. A moment of light-headedness slackened my lower body. To remain erect, I steadied myself against the wall until my blood resettled in its assigned organs.

These many years later, I recall leaving the chapel that late afternoon. I proceeded through the Vatican museum to the gate that sent me back into what some call the "real world." It was time to rejoin my wife whose failing health required her to rest during my excursions among the city's seemingly infinite antiquities. On my way back to our lodgings, a single question nagged at my spirit.

What is faith?

To find the answer, I had to search for something I had not previously acknowledged as missing. The spark of an answer arrived a week later, in one of those seemingly accidental moments I would later identify as an "actual grace."

My dear wife kept her Bible on our nightstand. In those latter days of her illness, I read to her. The calm tenor of my voice seemed to ease her discomfort. That evening, I pulled a rickety chair alongside her bed intending to read from the Gospel of John, her favorite.

Instead, the Bible fell open to Hebrews 11:1. I read just above a whisper:

"Faith is the assurance of what we hope for, being certain of what we cannot see."

I have quoted this verse before. I

beg your indulgence one more time.

In this darkest hour of my life, the God I believed in but hardly knew, offered me only intangible hope in my spiritual darkness. I choked back a desire to rail against divine cruelty that first allowed and now prolonged my beloved's illness. Suddenly, the eyes of my soul opened, and my now-attentive ears heard something new and quite wonderful:

Assurance

Hope

Being certain

Without proof

She looked into my tear-filled eyes and said, "Reading the Scriptures gives me hope that my suffering has meaning in God's greater plan." Her words rasped into a grating sound, forbidding others to escape before a spell of fitful coughing rendered further speech impossible. A deathly spray of blood spewed onto the clean white cloth I offered her.

"I am glad for that," was all I could utter from my flagging spirit. In that intimate moment, with tears rolling across my cheeks, I took my first step along the less-traveled road of faith. In doing so, I experienced an unfamiliar sense of . . . I can only call it . . . peace. Watching my beloved's life force recede in slow but irreversible retreat, I could not imagine what my own long and empty future might bring.

She did not sleep well during the night. Without appearing over-solicitous, I lay awake monitoring her every labored breath. With the dawn, her body seemed to relax—so did I. Was it too much to hope for a miraculous recovery? Her eruptions quieted to an occasional burst. She even slept a bit, or so it seemed.

She did not wake up.

All these years later, writing those last fateful words makes vivid again that worst moment of my young life.

I had lost my treasure. I was alone in the world for the first time ever, thousands of kilometers from France and home. Pondering from afar the despair I felt in my sudden emptiness, a poem now plays at the edges of my recall. Before retiring, I must record—for myself alone—what was in my heart that terrible night.

Loss

who suffers death more
living or deceased
pain of life
exceeds beloved's

loss of friend lover
amid reunion promises
buried bride of youth
my shining star

what of faith hope
promise of better life
i wander living hell
alone tormented

good host divine
delight in her
my goal in view
bereft's spirit anchor

sinks deep in sea
spirits rejoin hereafter
birth-designed pairing
living for reunion

Chapter the Fourteenth

First Letter to the Corinthians

Chapter 13

I confess to mixed feelings about my travels to distant parishes in my diocese. I do not enjoy the inevitable discomforts of the road. Am I still so much my father's son? As a child and youth, I traveled about Paris and the countryside in comfortable horsedrawn carriages. In my present capacity as bishop of the Diocese of Digne, I allow myself no more in the way of luxury on these visitations than that possessed by the people I serve.

From the beginning of my tenure, I have witnessed firsthand the needs of the struggling inhabitants of outlying regions in my largely mountainous diocese. I accept and cherish my role as servant to the priests and people who need connection with the larger Church beyond their villages and towns—locales some may never visit in their lifetimes. They rely on me to share, unbiased, news about matters of Church and State.

Conversely, they provide a salutary balance by sharing their earthy wisdom on a range of daily, real-life challenges they face. I also serve as a source of trustworthy news, as they seek information and clarification regarding rumors that have raced ahead of me into their forested heights.

Why do I venture alone on what others around me call "risky" journeys, sans companion or bodyguard? First, I do not wish to risk any life but my own. Second, there exist in yonder mountains small communities I may not have seen for two, sometimes three, years. I am their bishop. They are children of God and my dear friends, those gentle, honest people, a large number of whom are shepherds and goatherds. On the first Christmas night, did God the Father not send his angels first to shepherds, announcing the Good News of His son's birth?

Eighteen centuries later, I must not neglect God's favored folk. They have a right to hear about their good and loving God directly from their bishop. Not being an angelic visitor nor anything resembling a choir of angelic voices, I do my best to speak the truth in a clear voice.

I could send an emissary from among my senior clergy. But, I will not. I love watching the people at work, weaving pretty woolen cords dyed by their own hands in a variety of bright colors. I want to listen as they play their lovely mountain airs on six-hole flutes carved from Aromatic Red Cedar. What would they think of a bishop afraid to visit them, dine in their cottages, bring them Mass and Eucharist? Even should they forgive me, I could not forgive myself. I would not wish to carry that black mark on my soul when that final journey calls me back to the Good Shepherd who created me.

To reach my destination before a delayed summer sundown, I keep a steady pace, guiding my faithful mule along passages sometimes steep and rather narrow (not unlike the narrow path we tread on our way to virtuous living). With an eye to the sun's downward arc, I reflect on the thirteenth chapter of First Corinthians, on which I will base my sermon at our Solemn Mass together. This same text will bring to completion the final chapter of my book. Yes, its completion is in sight. Praise God!

Organizing and compiling the chapters of this work has consumed most of the past year. I must say it has proved a labor of love. I discovered that, should no eyes but mine—and my Lord's—ever peruse those pages, the writing itself emerges as its own reward. I dare to say that publication of *Duty* has faded into the mist of unimportance. I have written messages heard in my soul to my soul—the very words I myself needed to discover and live by.

Page by page, I experience less ownership of the script I see before think of a bishop afraid to visit them, dine in their cottages, bring them Mass and Eucharist? Even should they forgive me, I could not forgive myself.

I wonder, do other authors—inspired by their personal muses—gaze upon the printed products of their interior lives and see the work of a stranger, some creator other than themselves? Undaunted, I praise the Holy Spirit who guides my quill, giving the breath of life and meaning to each word, sentence, paragraph, and chapter, beyond any stated purpose of my own.

I lean forward in my jostling, basketlike chair (a *cacolet* we call it). Periodically, I stretch to run a soothing hand along my sullen mule's neck and whisper in his ear, "Thank you, faithful friend, for your selfless love and service."

The animal casts a quizzical look and plods on. I burst into laughter at my four-legged friend's expression. It says—if I may be granted an attempt at interpreting animal speech—"I cannot understand a word you are saying, but I do enjoy the sound of your voice, the touch of your gentle hand when you scratch my ears."

* * *

Alone now in my small but warm and comfortable bedroom, I reflect on the day quickly coming to an end. Upon my arrival, the local pastor came out of his bare-bones residence to welcome me. He confided that he had not conversed with a brother priest for many months. After a few hours of vigorous suppertime discussion, we opened and shared a healthy portion of local red wine, enhanced by subtle flavors of fertile highland soil and lush vegetation. When the weariness of the day's journey begged an end to conversation, I excused myself and surrendered to my need for solitude.

I remove my dusty, purple-piped soutane and retrieve a sheaf of blank pages from my valise. I am so tempted to replace them untouched. However, lest my balky memory fail me, I need to put in writing my reflection on Paul's inspired words. To me, his first letter to the Christian communities in and around the great city of Corinth, in Southern Greece, contains some of the most beautiful, soul-piercing text in the Scriptures—or anywhere.

Mustering my diminishing reserve of energy, I sit at a small desk resting below a window that I opened just enough to allow some fresh air to enter. A breath of gentle mountain breeze wafts over this sleepy-eyed, aging prelate, tempting him with the choice of sleep . . . but not prevailing. I feel a sudden wicked sense of freedom knowing Baptistine will not be present during my morning Mass to monitor and chronicle her brother's unstifled yawns.

For this unkind thought, forgive me, Lord.

As the decades raced onward, growing fewer in number, I dreamed of writing a book which might serve as my spiritual last will and testament . . . a summation of all that I believe and have striven to live by. For nearly a year, I have committed to paper my most cherished beliefs along with moments in my own life story, in which our Good Lord has wrapped my faith.

I intend to close this book with a meditation and teaching on my favorite chapter—among many—in the post-Resurrection Scriptures: the thirteenth chapter of St. Paul's First Letter to the Corinthians. I can think of no more appropriate way to end this flawed but sacred work.

How the Apostle to the Gentiles loved this community of mostly Greek-speaking converts! Within his soaring verses, he reveals the essence of his immense personal faith and generous heart beating with love and devotion for the companions with whom he has shared the highs and lows of his personal Christ journey. At the same time, Paul offers a spiritual guide for Christians of our time and beyond to follow, one that ensures safe arrival at our destined final dwelling.

"If I could speak all the human and angelic tongues, but had no

love, I would only be sounding
brass or a clanging cymbal." —v.1

Besides French, I speak Italian,
having gained some fluency during the
years of my chosen exile in Rome.
Some German, too, that I learned as a
young scholar in my university days. I
say this not to boast but to share a
lesson I learned early in my priestly
ministry. The majority of the patois-
speaking congregations I have served
derive little benefit from sermons rendered
in the pristine French spoken at court
and in Paris's Collège de Sorbonne.
As bishop of Digne, I learned early

on that I ranked in society just below the rank of Field Marshal. Without caring if that were an honor or an insult, I mentally divested myself of all titles and rights, both civil and ecclesiastical. I claimed a new identity as a provençal, a local, in mind, heart, and body.

Paris seemed a continent away, for which I was glad. Embracing my new environs, I dedicated myself to learning the dialect of the southern districts— Lower Languedoc, Lower Alps, and Upper Dauphiné.

I soon discovered that this earthy repertoire gave me greater access to the least educated of my flock. Addressing them in their familiar linguistic style and structure, enabled me to preach God's word with greater credibility, gentleness, and compassion—essential components of what Saint Paul referred to as "angelic tongues."

In turn, the populace responded with gratitude and affection. I even heard an occasional, "Our bishop, he is one of us," whispered sometimes but within my range of hearing.

If I could brag about speaking every language and dialect known to humankind, what merit would be mine? According to Paul, nothing. Love alone gives value to breath that becomes language.

"If I had the gift of prophecy, knowing secret things with all kinds of knowledge, and had faith great enough to remove mountains, but had no love, I would be nothing."—v. 2

Paul knew whereof he spoke. Religions everywhere and at all times become infested by so-called Gnostic teachers. They revel in "secret" knowledge possessed by only a chosen few—themselves—and canonize complexity. The more obtuse the message of "enlightenment" and "salvation," certainly the more divine it must be. Do they not know this most fundamental Christian truth: ours is a simple God, the o-n-e God? According to the Scriptures, self-inflation has been humanity's Achille's heel from the beginning of our race.

Herein lies the crux of the Genesis tragedy retold in Chapter 3. The serpent slithers up to Woman and whispers a hissing, "Trust me. If you eat the fruit of the Tree of Life, you will not die, as you've been told falsely by the master of this wonderous garden. He deceived you into this way of thinking. He knows well that, on the day you eat it, your eyes will be opened. Listen to me and you shall see secret things . . . and possess wisdom and knowledge beyond your imagining. Best of all, you will no longer be inferior to him. No, you will be gods . . . equal in every respect to your Creator."

Woman found the fruit quite lovely to look at. It promised a tasty treat more delicious than any other food available to them. No wonder the Creator did not want Woman and Man to gain full knowledge of all the mysteries of this wonderful, freshly minted world, their home. "How devious of Creator," the serpent suggests, "to withhold from you the best of Paradise! And to gain all knowledge—isn't that worth risking any unseen consequences of defying your maker?"

Adam and Eve read each other's eyes.

"What could God possibly do to us?" Eve asked her husband. "We share the power to create. Did God not told us so himself?"

Woman took the fruit . . . and ate . . . delicious. . . . She gave some to her husband. . . . He ate.

As promised, their eyes truly opened! And, what did they discover? For the first time, they saw . . . they truly saw with their own eyes the miracle of what they had always been but had no reason to acknowledge as a separate fact. They stood before each other . . . naked . . . and gloriously human . . . but not divine. Not in any sense equal to their Creator. It became their lot and that of their descendants to this day to learn and relearn the true meaning of love.

Eighteen centuries ago, in what Scripture refers to as "the fulness of time," Yahweh sent his own Son to this earth. Why? Not because love had failed, had proved too difficult for humans to preserve and pass on. The real truth? Not enough of the human race had given themselves to a generous, wholehearted pursuit of love.

Ah yes, to be sure, that one little word, l – o – v - e, found its way into every language spoken on earth. Sadly, every people in turn distorted that word from its divine meaning, translating it according to their personal, all too limited interpretations.

In my own lifetime, I have witnessed all manner of violence perpetrated for "love of country," "love of social class," "love of power" over anyone weaker, less powerful.

Jesus turned the tables on the desecration of Love by redefining its parameters. "Love your enemies, do good to those who hate you" (Luke 6:27).

Clinging to my Lord's model, at times by my fingernails, I avow that God has wrapped that precious gift in the utter simplicity of Paul's powerful words:

"If I gave everything I had to the poor . . . without love, it would be of no value to me."
— v. 3

I once heard one of my cathedral parishioners say to another, "When our bishop has money, he visits the poor; when he has none, he visits the rich."

I wish I had not heard this, but I confess to its truth. I do not boast. By the grace of God, I harbor no illusions about the virtue or value of my actions. A "reputation" for almsgiving does not equate with holiness, nor assure one a place at the right hand of our heavenly Father.

Making a show of profligate charity disguises self-aggrandizing benevolence. It has the contrary effect of bringing no more than diminished value to the donor. In the second verse, sixth chapter, of Saint Matthew's Gospel, Jesus says, "When you give something to the poor, do not have it trumpeted before you."

Our Lord concludes with a bit of holy sarcasm, "They have their reward." That "reward" resides in the fleeting notoriety and any flattering praise the donor might receive.

Any value such good works possess lies in their momentary relief of suffering. No small thing, I admit.

Better mercy for a flawed reason than prolonged and unrelenting suffering for the poor. In my daily examen, I search my conscience for traces of self-deceit and utter a prayer for purity of intention in all that I say and do.

"Love is patient, kind, without

envy. It is not boastful or arrogant. It is not ill-mannered, nor does it seek its own interest. Love overcomes anger and forgets offenses. . . ."—v. 4

Who does not struggle with patience and kindness? Who does not fail at times? My own domestic situation, with sole care of an elderly spinster and a widow, challenges me to live with women whom I treasure, even as they fuss all too much over my daily care and well-being.

In my more objective moments, I understand that their protective stance is for their good as much as mine. What would become of them should I die? Especially now that I have surrendered our family heirlooms to a stranger in the person of Jean Valjean, a man whose name is as permanently tattooed on my heart, as 24601 stained that poor benighted soul's body. Can I rely on Holy Mother Church to assume Baptistine's support in gratitude for decades of service to this poor bishop, her brother? I hope—and pray—it will be so. At the same time, I worry about the opposite.

"Love will never end."—v. 8

Paul's assertion about the primacy of love exposes the lie of popular belief that evil triumphs over goodness. If I could halt the progress of time and examine French society today, what would I find?

Rampant corruption at all levels

Undeserved misery

Gross injustice

Rivalries and hatreds often ending in senseless death

Abuse of power

Unspeakable forms of human trafficking and sexual perversion

All that and worse, if anything could

be worse.

Measured against this deadening weight of human weakness, pockets of virtue illumine our French landscape. Monasteries keep holiness, knowledge, and wisdom alive. Religious communities of women, like our Sisters of Charity of St. Vincent de Paul, labor day and night in our hospital caring for the sick and dying. A good number of charitable women and men volunteer their services with great generosity. Dedicated priests give themselves to selfless service—in the majority of our parishes, at least. Above all, mothers and fathers who received the Christian faith from their parents now pass that life-lighting torch to their children. I number all these among France's true heroes. Never will anyone build a monument to honor them. No gold-framed portraits will hang in Paris's Louvre as tribute to their lives.

Because of them and their predecessors in sacrificial faith, the gospel of Jesus Christ has survived down the centuries. They continue to inspire men and women to strive for virtuous living, often under the most difficult circumstances. These are "the last," who "shall be first" in the kingdom of God, as Matthew 20:16

cites in the Lord's parable about the workers in the vineyard. I praise our God whose light and love will never disappear from the earth.

"Now we have faith, hope, and love, these three, but the greatest of these is love." —v. 13

All creation shall pass. Even this lovely mountain beneath my feet, with its base of granite as old as time itself and its annual regeneration of native vegetation. Like my own existence, this mountain's life suffers a finite timeline. "When" and "how" my and this landscape's deaths shall occur, I dare not speculate.

In Italy, the end of my "everything" caused the internal paralysis I experienced in the months following the loss of my beloved spouse and best friend. As a new priest, my inability to share freely my undulled sorrow inflicted a great personal test, upon my return to France. Those with intimate knowledge of my "other" life assumed that the grace of my call to Orders had miraculously healed my heartache. I chose to let them think so, as long as they did not witness the tears that welled up in my few unguarded moments.

At the end of this life, I shall gladly leave behind my ecclesiastical titles. I have little use for them even now. Still, the thought of approaching death fills me with a mixture of joy and dread. With advancing age, an awareness has evolved that I have peppered my life with half measures, missed opportunities. I take comfort in the fact that only two human beings—the man-God Jesus Christ and the Virgin Mary, his mother—ever returned unblemished to the home of Father-God.

And so, I fervently pray each day, "Lord, have mercy on me, a sinner." The inevitability of death does not disturb me, although I do have a preference about the when and how. Not soon, I hope, since I have two women to provide for. How do I imagine my "perfect" death scene? To begin, I pray that Baptistine will have preceded me into eternity. And Madame Magloire has returned to live out her days with her family.

I see myself in our hospital in Digne. White-habited nuns come and go, doing what they can to comfort me in my final hours. In parish churches, the good people of my diocese pray for their bishop's safe passage home. A crypt in the cathedral floor awaits me.

An artisan will carve my name upon

the stone and, perhaps, an all too flattering epitaph.

How mortifying it would be to have my Lord and Savior Jesus, the Risen Christ, welcome me home with the title, "Your Excellency."

The only words I long to hear are these, from St. Matthew's image of the Final Judgment: "Well done, good and faithful servant. Since you have been faithful in a few things, I will entrust you in charge of many things. Come and share the joy of your master" (25:21).

The End — Draft No. 1

Ghostwriter's Afterword

Was It Only a Dream?

Victor Hugo wrote no deathbed scene for Bishop Myriel. His last "sighting" in the novel is in a vision witnessed solely by Jean Valjean in the final moments of his heroic life. Hugo describes that scene in these tender, reverential words . . .

> *The portress had come upstairs and was gazing in at the half-open door. The doctor dismissed her. But he could not prevent this zealous woman from exclaiming to the dying man before she disappeared: "Would you like a priest?"*
>
> *"I have had one," replied Jean Valjean. And with his finger he seemed to indicate a point above his head where one would have said that he saw someone. It is probable, in fact, that the Bishop was present at this death agony.*
>
> Jean Valjean, Book the Ninth, V,
> Night Behind Which is Dawn

. . . with that the curtain falls on Valjean's life . . .

In the cemetery of Pere-Lachaise, in the vicinity of the common grave, far from the elegant quarter of that city of sepulchers, far from all the tombs of fancy which display in the presence of eternity all the hideous fashions of death, in a deserted corner, beside an old wall, beneath a great yew tree over which climbs the wild convolvulus, amid dandelions and mosses, there lies a stone. That stone is no more exempt than others from the leprosy of time, of dampness, of the lichens and from the defilement of the birds. The water turns it green, the air blackens it. It is not near any path, and people are not fond of walking in that direction, because the grass is high, and their feet are immediately wet. When there is a little sunshine, the lizards come thither. All around there is a quivering of weeds. In the spring, linnets warble in the trees.

This stone is perfectly plain. In cutting it the only thought was the requirements of the tomb, and no other care was taken than to make

*the stone long enough and narrow enough to
cover a man.*

No name is to be read there.

How does Hugo end his twelve-hundred-page
masterpiece? With a mystical poem an unknown
stranger has written—in pencil!—on Jean Valjean's
unmarked tombstone.

> *Only, many years ago, a hand wrote upon
> (the stone) in pencil these lines, which have
> become gradually illegible beneath the rain
> and the dust, and which are, today, probably
> effaced:*
>
> *He sleeps.*
> *Although his fate*
> *was very strange, he lived.*
> *He died when he had*
> *no longer his angel.*
> *The thing came to pass simply,*
> *of itself, as the night comes*
> *when day is gone.*

Jean Valjean, Book the Ninth, Chapter VI,
Grass Hides and Rain Blots Out

The catching up and storytelling that followed in Afterlife—Valjean and Myriel meeting again, once and forever with mutual joy. . . .

That is a scene we can only imagine . . . with envy. Eternity might not be time enough for each to share his stories.

Hugo's Model for Bishop Myriel

We cannot end this story without saying that, for *Les Miserables*, Victor Hugo modeled his fictional Bishop Charles Francois Myriel after the real Bishop of Digne, Francois Melchior Charles de Miollis (1773-1843).

Both Myriel and Miollis had fathers who were councilors. Hugo even overlapped the dates and places of their episcopal tenures in Digne. Both had the same nickname, Bienvenu (meaning "welcome"), due to their charitable natures and evangelical virtues. Myriel used his inherited silver candlesticks to redeem Jean Valjean. After the French Revolution, Miollis used his personal funds to redeem the church and the presbytery of Notre Dame du Laus.

A significant difference between the two is found in Hugo's decision to have his bishop married and widowed prior to ordination as a priest. Bishop de Miollis never married.

Hugo wrote: "(Bishop Myriel's) father had arranged a marriage for his son. In spite of this marriage, however, it was said that Charles Myriel created a great deal of talk. He was well formed, though rather short in stature, elegant, graceful, intelligent; the whole of the first portion of his life had been devoted to the world and to gallantry."

About the Author

Alfred J. Garrotto is a confessed and unabashed Hugophile.

A native of a beautiful beach city, Santa Monica in Southern California, he now resides in the San Francisco East Bay Area. He was born into a theatrical family and began his career in the arts at the age of seven, along with older sister Natalie, doing (non-speaking) bit parts in movies requiring "Italian-looking kids." She used her magnificent coloratura voice to pursue a career in grand opera. Their younger sister, Toni, has sung and acted with Los Angeles area theater groups.

By his teens, the middle child had taken a different road into academics and spirituality. Over the years, he did a great deal of writing and teaching (mostly on Christian themes), he did not get the book-length bug until his forties. Once the muse struck, he couldn't stop and has written, to date, thirteen books through both commercial and independent publishing channels. These include both fiction and nonfiction.

The author's passion for Victor Hugo's masterwork (in all its iterations) led him to write *The Wisdom of Les Miserables: Lessons from the Heart of Jean Valjean* (2008) to which *Bishop Myriel: In His Own Words* is the sequel. His hope is to complete the trilogy with *Inspector Javert*.

His novella, *There's More*, explores the greatest mystery of all: what happens at the instant of death? In it, a major league ballplayer—and former Catholic priest—is simultaneously murdered and killed by accident, by two different people, during a World Series game! The plot explores questions about death and afterlife, as the ballplayer-priest reviews major moments and decisions of his life, under the guidance of none other than Bishop Charles Francois Myriel, Victor Hugo's catalyst character in *Les Miserables*.

His most recent fiction works are the romantic thriller Caribbean Tremors Trilogy(2019).: *A Love Forbidden, Finding Isabella, I'll Paint a Sun.*

In his nonfiction work, *The Soul of Art* (2016), the author explores the underlying spirituality that gives birth to all creative endeavors. The book inspired his "Spirituality of the Arts" workshops designed for creative people of all genres. You can contact him by email for further details and possible bookings at:

algarrotto@comcast.net.

The author invites you to visit his blog: https://wisdomoflesmiserables.blogspot.com/.

You will also find him on Facebook (AlfredJGarrottoAuthor),

and on Twitter *@algarrotto*.

Acknowledgements

I am particularly indebted to my friend and colleague Judith Ingram, author of *Forgiving Day by Day: Practicing God's Ways in Our Relationships*, for her back-cover quote. I urge you to read her novels and nonfiction spiritual books on the theme of forgiveness.

I have already mentioned the wise contributions of Honey O'Leary, in the Ghostwriter's Preface. In addition, I am deeply indebted to my other generous beta readers, Jim Gallagher, and Natalie and Andrei Tremaine for their time in plowing through early drafts of this book and offering helpful comments and suggestions.

I am also grateful to photographer Matthew T. Rader whose candle image appears on the front cover. I highly recommend the royalty-free photo gallery at Unsplash. com. I have used a number of images from that site in my books and trailers.

Finally, I am grateful to my understanding and supportive wife, Esther, for allowing me to disappear into my office for hours on end while writing this book. She's the very best, believe me!